I Can Do It Better

I Can Do It Better

Rob Matthews

Seattle, WA

Fanny Press
PO Box 70515
Seattle, WA 98127

For more information go to: www.fannypress.com

Cover design by Sabrina Sun

I Can Do It Better
Copyright © 2016 by Rob Matthews

ISBN: 978-1-60381-457-7 (Trade Paper)
ISBN: 978-1-60381-460-7 (eBook)

Printed in the United States of America

Thanks to Catherine Treadgold and everyone at Fanny Press for their help and support with A Cuckold Odyssey.

Also by the Author

Come Home With Us

Chapter One

~

'DON'T *EVER FEEL GUILTY*,' said Tina. 'Remember, your man wants this as much as you do. But let me give you one piece of advice: don't fall in love.'

Emma smiled. 'There's not much danger of that. I love Ben.'

'And I love Rob, but having great sex can mess with your head.'

On a Friday evening in July, the four of us were sitting round the table in our dining room. We'd finished eating. Emma and Ben had brought three bottles of Les Chaillots Burgundy. It was more expensive than the stuff Tina and I normally drank, so I sipped it slowly. Tina, on the other hand, was enjoying this taste of the high life and gulping it down. Emma was matching her glass for glass.

Emma was twenty-five, with an accent and a self-confidence you can only get at an English private school. She looked the part of an English rose as well—slim with small breasts, her black hair bobbed below her jaw line, dark brown eyes and a deep groove in her upper lip. The only out-of-place element was a bump on the bridge of her nose. Some might have called it an imperfection, but I thought it gave her face more character. She was sophisticated, but with a hint of wildness. Her boyfriend Ben was obviously crazy about her and I could see why. I could imagine her charming his mom over dinner while she jerked him off under the table. My cock stirred at the thought, and I had to shake myself back to reality. Ben sat next to her, a boyishly handsome rich kid—tall and slight with sandy hair that flopped over his forehead. His eyes were green and his brows looped up higher than normal, giving him a permanently surprised expression. Or maybe he *was* perpetually surprised to be with someone like Emma.

It was the first time we'd met them face to face. I'd have preferred to get together in a public place but Tina had sent Emma our address without giving it too much thought. So far, they weren't showing any psychotic tendencies. And I was reassured by our dog's reaction to them. Boris had good instincts about people. If our Labrador-based mongrel barked at someone, there was always a reason. When Emma and Ben had arrived, he'd sniffed them and let Emma rub his chest. Then he'd lain down under the table.

Tina carried on, 'It was where I went wrong with Steve, my last stud. We were having mind-blowing sex, so I reckoned I must be in love with him. I even thought I wanted to live with him, which was a huge mistake.' She reached across the table and squeezed my hand. 'Rob's the love of my life. I should never have doubted that. You can have fantastic sex with someone you hate. You can also be completely in love with someone even if the sex isn't all that great.' She patted my hand in a slightly condescending way.

Emma looked at Ben. 'I can vouch for that.'

'Enjoy everything the stud does for you.' She pointed her finger at Emma to drive home the most important point. 'But love the cuck, not the stud. And always remember—'

'Have you met anyone else from the site?' asked Emma.

Tina frowned, took a mouthful of wine and said, 'No. I've had plenty of offers. Most of them were from sad little men who said, "Please, may I worship and adore you?" I have Rob for that. I've also chatted with a few women—or people who said they were women.'

'Did you think I was a man?'

'No, you were different from the start. Guys always ask me hundreds of detailed questions. "What type of lingerie do you wear when you go out with the expectation of meeting a man for extramarital sex? Give size, color, and brand. Do you allow other men to kiss you—if so, is it on the lips and are tongues permitted?" You actually wanted to talk about yourself.'

Ben had been quiet up until now. He'd spent most of the time giving Boris scraps off his plate while Tina and Emma were talking. Now he leaned forward and said, 'Can I be one of those typical men and ask you a detailed question?'

'Sure,' said Tina.

'What are you doing differently with the guy you're seeing …?' He paused and looked at Tina. 'Are you happy to talk about these things? I mean, it's personal stuff.'

Tina spread her hands. 'Hey, we're all friends here.'

Apart from a few chats on a website, we'd known them for a little over an hour. I wasn't sure we were best buds yet.

'We can agree that nothing leaves this room,' said Tina.

'What are you doing differently with this guy? I'm guessing you didn't *want* to fall in love with Steve.'

'We've learnt a lot,' said Tina. 'Kieran doesn't kiss me on the lips. He doesn't stay the night. Also, he's … Kieran. He's nice enough but ….' She shrugged. 'Sex with Kieran is like drinking water. I need it to live, but it's not very exciting.'

'What do you mean?'

* * *

Two months earlier ….

TINA LET OUT A small groan of disappointment when Kieran walked into the coffee shop. 'That's him,' she said.

'Are you sure?' I asked. 'I thought he had dark hair.'

'Maybe Goths "R" Us ran out of dye.'

'He looks okay.'

'But nothing special. All his pictures on Facebook must be ten years old.'

'We can sneak out the side door if you want.'

'No, he came here to meet us. The least we can do is buy him a cappuccino.' She managed to give me something close to her wicked grin. 'Anyway, his main selling point did not come out of a bottle.' She held up her hand and waved. 'Kieran! Over here!'

He was wearing a light gray suit over an open-collared white shirt. He was just short of albino. I wondered if he was from Ireland or some other perpetually cloudy place. Aside from his pale skin, he had short blond hair and blue eyes. Five minutes in the sun would have turned him into a cherry tomato.

'Tina,' he said, shaking her hand, 'it's good to see you again.'

'You too,' she said. 'This is Rob.'

'Err … yes,' he said, smiling at me uncomfortably. He sat down.

'How have you been?' she asked him.

'Not bad,' he said. 'You haven't changed much.'

'You have.'

'In a good way, I hope?'

She didn't want to answer that one, so she asked, 'What are you doing these days?'

'I work for a garden products company. You know those robotic lawnmowers you see in rich folks' gardens? I train the people who sell them.'

'Did the boss make you lose the vampire look?'

'The what? Oh, that was just a phase when I was a student. What do *you* do?'

'Guess.'

'Actress?'

Tina laughed. 'That would be interesting, but I'm a manager

in a firm of civil engineering consultants.'

'Your company is fairly liberal when it comes to hairstyles?' he said, looking at Tina's spikes.

'I can flatten them down when I have to. It's more conservative at your place?'

' "If we don't keep ourselves neat, how can people trust us with the neatness of their lawns?" That's what my boss says—two or three times a day.'

'Your girlfriend doesn't mind the preppy look?'

'No, she likes it.'

'Trapped you. Your Facebook status says you're single.'

A sly smile. 'She's not really my girlfriend.'

'That old line.'

'She likes going to the movies. Afterwards, she wants to drink wine and talk about what she's seen. I'm happy to watch, drink, and talk. I enjoy eating in restaurants and the words, "Table for one" always sound a bit sad.'

'Convenient arrangement.'

'You two,' he began, 'you're married, right?'

'Sixteen years now.'

'So …?'

'Why is a decent married woman messaging a guy she hasn't seen in ages?' Tina said with a smile.

'Yes.'

'Particularly as we weren't really friends or anything; we just fooled around one time?' She paused a moment and swirled the coffee in her cup. Once again, she was discovering there's no easy way to tell a man you want him to fuck you while your husband watches. 'Well … I'm sorry we never got to know each other properly.'

That didn't sound convincing, but he might have been offended if she'd said, 'I'm sorry I never got your huge cock inside me because I had my period last time we met.'

Instead, she said, 'I should have gotten in touch with you again. But you know how it goes. And also,' she took another mouthful of coffee as she tried to find the right words, 'Rob and I are totally in love and we still have a passionate relationship. How many couples can say that after sixteen years? One of the things that keeps the fire burning is … the involvement of other people.'

'Involvement?' He scratched his head.

Tina sighed quietly. I think she was wondering how obvious she had to be. 'I have sex with other men.'

Kieran raised his eyebrows at me. 'You're okay with that?'

Tina answered for me, 'He loves it.'

He grimaced. 'Why?'

'That's something Rob can work through with a good analyst,' she said. 'For now, I'm happy to have the best of both worlds. I have a loving relationship with my husband. I can also have fun with other guys. And we were wondering—'

'If I'd be one of the guys you have fun with?' His expression didn't give away anything. Tina looked relieved that he'd finally got the point.

There was a silence that went on too long.

'What do you think?' she asked finally.

He looked at the table. 'I don't know. It's a lot to take in.'

'It won't stop you seeing other people. We can call it a day whenever you want.'

'I mean, you're very pretty and everything ….' He looked at her, then at me.

'It won't be a problem, I promise,' she said.

'Can I think about it for a while?' I could tell he was attracted to Tina by the way his eyes roamed over her, but something—probably me—was bothering him.

'If you like. Or maybe we could try it once—see how it goes? If it doesn't work out, no hard feelings. Maybe try again in another nineteen years.'

He cleared his throat. 'I do need some time. I'm not sure this is my scene.' He stood up. 'Well, it was good to catch up. Nice to meet you ….'

'Rob.'

'I'll be in touch,' he said, and walked out of the shop rather more quickly than necessary.

'No, you won't,' muttered Tina, as the door closed behind him. She slumped down in her chair. 'Rob, am I still sexy? Be honest.'

'Are you kidding? You're gorgeous.'

'I offered it to him—no strings attached. And he couldn't get out fast enough.'

I caressed her neck. 'There might be any number of reasons. Perhaps that girlfriend isn't as casual as he says. Or, with a name like Kieran, maybe he's a devout Catholic. He's worried about what his priest would say.'

'He wasn't thinking about his priest when he fucked my tits on his bedroom floor.'

'You weren't married then.'

'Or I'm not the girl I was.'

'He's not the same, either," I said, finding it hard to reconcile this pale worker bee with the edgy goth she'd described. 'You were disappointed when you saw him.'

'I was. So it should have been *me* rejecting *him*. But I decided, out of the goodness of my heart, to give him a go. And he turned me down.' She shook her head dejectedly. 'Come on, babe, let's go home. I may have to face the fact that you're the only one who still finds me attractive.'

WHEN WE GOT BACK to the house, we went to bed. This wasn't a time for fantasizing. It was a time for reassurance. I slowly undressed her, tenderly kissing every part of her body. When she was down to her underwear, I laid her gently on the bed. I spent a long time kissing her neck, then took off her bra. 'Beautiful,' I said. I wasn't faking it. Those natural 34C breasts were perfect. I kissed my way down her stomach until I reached her thighs, nuzzling her cunt through her panties. She lifted her ass off the bed so I could slide her panties down. I licked her clit. I wanted to make her cum with my tongue, but she said, 'I need more.'

There was an open packet of condoms by the bed. I put one on and lay on top of her. After she put my cock inside her, I held her tight and enjoyed the feeling of closeness. When I kissed her on the lips, she opened her mouth and my tongue found hers. I gazed into her eyes as I said, 'You're the loveliest, sexiest woman I've ever seen. I'm filled with pride every time we go out. People are so jealous when they see me with you. Right now, I feel like the luckiest bastard in the world because I'm the one making love with you.'

I kissed her again and started to fuck her. I tried thinking about politicians, but it didn't work. It took me less than two minutes to cum.

'Even after all these years, you still can't control yourself with me,' she said. She almost made that sound like a good thing. I lay beside her and put two fingers into her cunt. I moved them in and out slowly while my thumb massaged her clit. All the time, I told her how beautiful she was and how much I loved her. I brought her to a quiet but intense orgasm. 'Thank you, babe,' she said.

Chapter Two

~

T HE NEXT EVENING, WE were watching television when her phone beeped. 'Facebook message,' she said. She touched the screen a couple of times, then passed her phone to me.

Dear Tina, It was good to meet you and your husband the other day. The more I think about your suggestion, the more interested I am. I was wondering if you're free on Wednesday. If so, maybe I could come round to your place. I look forward to seeing you again soon. Best regards, Kieran

'No one's ever asked me for a fuck more politely,' she said.

'You see?' I said, handing the phone back to her. 'You haven't lost it. He just needed time to get his nerve up.'

She was already typing her reply.

Dear Kieran, That would be most agreeable. We'll be pleased to welcome you at seven o'clock on Wednesday. Cordially, Tina

A minute later, her phone beeped again.

If it's not too much trouble, could you wear stockings— preferably white?

She shrugged. 'I'm sure we can manage that.'

'Have you got any white stockings?'

'I bought some for Steve, but they're a bit worn. Kieran deserves a new pair.'

'You mean we have to waste an evening going into town?'

She gave me her wicked look. 'Or, to put it another way, we're going to buy something so I can turn on another man. You're going to pay for it. Do you like that idea better? We also need to buy super-size condoms. The ones you use won't even fit over the head of his cock.' She put her hand on my crotch and grinned as she felt how hard her words made me.

'Okay, we'll go tomorrow,' I said.

So, AT SEVEN O'CLOCK on Wednesday, Kieran came round for the first time. He was wearing the same gray suit. Boris went up to him, sniffed, and padded off without offering an opinion one way or the other. We took Kieran into the den.

'Would you like some wine?' I asked him.

'I'm driving.'

'I can make coffee if you want.'

'I'd better not. I have trouble sleeping if I drink coffee after midday. I wouldn't mind a glass of water, though.'

'It's going to be a wild and crazy night,' I muttered to Tina as I went out. She smirked.

When I came back, he said, 'I've got an early start tomorrow, so maybe we could ….' He wasn't sure how to finish that sentence. He patted his thighs nervously. 'How are we going to do this?'

'We've decided we'd better not kiss on the lips,' she said.

'No problem.'

'Apart from that, pretty much anything goes.'

She took his hand and led him up the stairs. I followed with mixed feelings. In some ways, this scene was too familiar. It reminded me of the first time she'd taken Steve upstairs. I couldn't help remembering how that had turned out. On the other hand, I was excited. My wife was going to have sex with another man again. And I'd heard so much about Kieran's cock, I was keen to see if the stories were true.

Tina switched on the light in the bedroom. Reaching behind her back, she unzipped her dress—a strapless number in red crushed velvet. However many times I saw it, I never got blasé about watching my wife undressing for another man. She was letting him look at her in a way that should have been reserved for me. He gasped—and so did I—when she let her dress fall to the floor. She was wearing the white stockings with a matching bra. And nothing else. The suspenders, belt, and stocking tops were a perfect frame for her cunt.

Kieran looked at her for a moment. 'Wow,' was all he said.

'Now you,' she said. He hung his jacket on the bedpost. His shirt, trousers and socks came off next. He was neither too fat nor too thin. His skin was paper white with freckles on the shoulders. Apart from a blond tuft under each arm, he had no hair on his upper body.

Tina held her breath as he pulled down his shorts. Maybe his cock wouldn't be as big as she remembered. She needn't have worried. 'I think it's actually grown,' she said quietly. 'And it's still beautiful.' It *was* the ten-incher of our fantasies, with twice the girth of mine. Why was he wasting his talent in a garden products company? He could have walked onto the set of any porn film and instantly become a legend. She put her hands on it. She didn't rub it or stimulate it, just felt it all over, as if she wanted to check if it was real.

She got onto the bed and lay on her back. Slowly, she spread her legs. He gazed, open-mouthed, at her cunt and bent down to part the lips gently with his thumbs, exposing the coral pink of her labia and then the warm red of her vagina. He lowered his head and kissed her clit.

He lay down on the bed beside her.

'Bra on or off?' she asked.

'Off, please.'

She sat up and undid the hooks.

'Wow,' he said again, as he gazed at my wife's beautiful tits.

'Everything you remember?' she asked. 'Why don't you fuck them a little, for old time's sake?'

Supporting himself on the headboard, he got into position to straddle her chest. He put his cock between her tits and she pushed them together. As he felt her soft flesh against his hardness, he closed his eyes.

'Do you know something?' she said. 'Every time a man's fucked my tits since you did it, I've said he's Kieraned me. So I've been thinking of you every time.'

Looking up, she saw the ecstasy on his face. She smiled proudly but didn't want him to get too excited. 'That's enough,' she said. 'You've got another job to do today.'

He moved down her body and licked her cunt. 'Don't worry,' she said. 'I'm ready for you.' She held out her hand to me. I gave her one of the extra-large condoms we'd bought. She put it on him and he got on top of her. Taking hold of his cock, she positioned it at the entrance to her cunt. 'Now, go slowly, Kieran,' she said. 'I've never had a cock like yours before.'

'If it hurts, tell me, and we'll stop.'

'Okay. Try it.' He pushed the head of his cock into her. She breathed in sharply, but not with pain. It was more like surprise at feeling the mouth of her cunt being stretched. 'That's good,' she said, as surprise gave way to pleasure. He went in deeper. She spread her legs wider, opening herself up a little more. Finally, he was all the way inside.

'Does that feel all right?' he asked.

'A lot better than all right,' she breathed.

He started moving inside her. His lips gravitated towards hers, but she remembered to turn her head away, and he kissed her neck instead. He fucked her slowly at first. When he was sure he wasn't hurting her, he thrust with more force. Now he knew she could take it all, he made her feel every inch. While his cock was pumping into her hard, his lips were lightly brushing against her neck and throat. She moaned with pleasure.

As I watched, I felt the usual dizzying mix of emotions. I

hated him for taking my place and doing what I should have been doing. I also loved him a little bit for giving my wife so much pleasure. I was proud of her for being so gorgeous and sexy. But part of me was angry with her. She was supposed to love me and me alone. So why was she doing this with another guy?

Kieran kept going with no sign of tiring or slowing down. He was obviously intent on making her cum with his cock. It worked. A flush rose from her breast to her throat, her head rocked back on the pillow, and she closed her eyes. The noise she made when she came was like a sigh of relief. Her body relaxed.

He waited until she opened her eyes, then asked, 'Is it okay if I …?'

'You've earned the right to cum wherever you want.'

He took the condom off and laid it neatly on the bed. It was the size of a sock. Straddling her chest again, he placed his cock back in her cleavage. She tilted her head forwards so she could see his huge cock head going in and out between her breasts.

He fucked her tits for five minutes before pulling out and kneeling beside her. Then, taking his cock in his right hand, he aimed. She pushed her tits together to make a target. 'Fifty points for a nipple, twenty-five for an outer,' she said with a grin. He stroked his cock. It wasn't long before he groaned and came in two great gushes. The first one covered both her tits, scoring him a hundred and fifty points by my reckoning. The second covered her midriff and filled her bellybutton.

There was an awkward, "What do we do now?" moment. He knelt down as his erection slowly subsided. She lay there, covered in semen. I broke the ice by giving her a tissue. 'Err … babe,' she said, looking down at her chest and stomach. I gave her all the tissues in the box.

'Any chance I could have a tissue?' Kieran asked. His cock and his right hand were glistening. Even in repose, his cock was the size of a young badger. He'd need more than one tissue to get that clean. I opened a new box and handed him a wad.

He stood up and looked at Tina, then at me. 'As I was saying,' he began, 'early start tomorrow. I'd better—'

'That's fine,' she said, wiping her neck to catch some stray splashes. 'Thanks for … err … coming.'

He dressed quickly. Tina stayed in bed while I showed him out. At the door, he turned to me and said, 'Was that all right?'

'You did great,' I said, feeling like the boss encouraging the new guy.

He gave me a relieved smile and held out his hand. I shook it and could feel it was still sticky. I waved him off and went into the kitchen to wash my hands.

Tina was still in bed when I got back upstairs. She had pushed her tits together again and was playing with her nipples. 'How was that for you?' I asked her, as I started undressing.

'That was good,' she said. 'Did you see his cock?'

'I couldn't miss it. The biggest you've ever had?'

'Definitely. I wasn't sure if I could take it. But I did. Your wife had every inch of that massive cock in her slutty pussy.'

'How did it feel?'

'He touched parts of me no man has ever reached before.'

'He's got big balls too.'

'Believe me, I noticed. I waited nineteen years to feel them bumping up against my ass.'

'They were very full.'

She grinned. 'Well, they aren't anymore. It was like standing under a waterfall. If he's going to visit us regularly, we'll be Kleenex's best customers.'

'Did you get it all cleaned up?' I asked.

'Not quite,' she said, with a sly look. She took her hands away from her chest and her tits parted. There was a small puddle of semen in her cleavage. 'I saved some for you.'

To think I'd been squeamish about having his cum on my hand …. I was never sure how I felt about this part of being a cuckold. There was something intensely exciting about the *idea* of licking another man's cum off my wife—especially an intimate part of her. The *reality* was a warm and sticky goo that didn't taste too good. And I could always feel it coating the back of my throat for hours afterwards.

But Tina loved it so I lay down beside her. 'Make sure you get every drop, babe,' she said. It was like taking medicine. I closed my eyes and swallowed it as quickly as possible. Her moans of arousal as I lapped it up made my task a lot easier. After I'd finished, I moved up the bed and kissed her. She opened her mouth and pushed her tongue against mine. She liked the taste more than I did. 'What do you want to do now?' she asked. My cock was hard—so I wasn't *too* turned off by what I'd just done. I pressed it against her thigh. She smiled. 'You want to fuck me?'

'Of course. Unless you're too sore.'

'I'm not sure I could take *his* cock again. *Yours* will be fine. Come on, babe, see if you can follow that.'

Obviously, I couldn't follow that. But I put on one of my condoms and got on top of her. When I was inside, she pushed my face into her chest and said, 'Smell the other man's semen on your wife's tits.'

She knew this would be too much for me. As I felt myself cumming, I said, 'Oh, no!' She laughed, but not in a nasty way. She *sometimes* finds it funny when I can't control myself.

I went down and started licking her cunt. 'Oh yes!' she said. I badly wanted to make her cum. The fuck from me was nothing compared to what Kieran had given her, but I wanted to be at least a footnote in her memories of this evening. She could look back and think, 'After Kieran left, my husband gave me another earth-shattering orgasm.' I put her clit between my lips and fluttered my tongue against it as fast as I could. It wasn't long before her body stiffened and then relaxed. It wasn't as intense as the cum she'd had with Kieran inside her, but she gave a moan of satisfaction. I moved back up her body. She was smiling happily.

She laid her head on my chest and I put my arms around her. Whatever she did with anyone else, I was still her husband. I was the one who held her. 'What are we having for supper?' she asked.

'Nachos,' I said.

'Cool. Do you want to put those on? I'll go and make it up with Boris.'

We got out of bed, put our clothes on, and went downstairs.

As I grated cheese onto the nachos, I heard Tina talking to Boris. 'Sorry we had to shut you out, honey. There are some things you don't want to see.'

After the cheese had melted, I put the nachos on a big plate with guacamole and soured cream. I brought the plate into the den and sat on the couch next to Tina. Boris lay down at my feet and gobbled up the chunk of cheese I'd saved for him.

'How was that for you?' asked Tina, scooping up guacamole with a handful of nachos.

'Pretty much perfect,' I said. 'He arrived. He made *you* cum. He made *me* jealous. He left straight afterwards. We get to spend a quiet evening, just the two of us—'

'Just the three of us,' said Tina, patting Boris's head.

'Of course. Sorry, buddy. What I meant is we don't have some guy sitting around wondering how long he has to make polite conversation before he can fuck you again. And he has some sort of girlfriend, so he's not so likely to fall in love with you.'

'We've cracked it, babe.'

We held up our glasses. It was mid-week and we were trying to be good, so they were full of apple juice. We clinked them together and drank a toast to our ideal arrangement.

THE NEXT DAY, TINA went into her Facebook account and saw a message from Kieran.

Thank you for a lovely evening. I was wondering if you're free next Wednesday. Maybe we could do the same thing again.

So the next Wednesday, they did the same thing—*exactly*

the same. He wanted her to wear the same white stockings. He arrived. He drank a glass of water. We went upstairs. He fucked Tina. He made her cum. He fucked her tits for a while. He came all over her. He left.

For me, it was still the optimal setup. I got to watch my wife with another man. Then I got to spend time alone with her. She talked about his cock and how good it felt. Sometimes she compared mine unfavorably to his. We had sex and then we had a regular evening together. Tina seemed to like it too.

Before he came round the Wednesday after that, she asked me to close the drapes in the den and put Boris in the kitchen. She took her clothes off so that when Kieran arrived, she was sitting on the couch, wearing nothing except his beloved white stockings. 'How do I look?' she asked him.

'Awesome,' he said. 'I can't wait to get you upstairs.'

'About that,' she said, patting the arm of the couch. 'This one time, a guy fucked me right here.'

'I think we'll be more comfortable in the bed.'

'Maybe we could start here and go up to the bedroom later?'

'I think we'll be more comfortable in the bed,' he repeated.

He headed up the stairs, and we had no choice but to follow him. Tina wasn't done trying to shake things up, though. She got onto the bed on all fours. He knelt on the bed behind her and stroked her ass. She moaned with approval and pushed her butt up towards him. Then he gently but firmly flipped her over so she was lying on her back. 'Don't you want to fuck me from behind?' she asked.

'I want to look at your lovely face.'

She couldn't deny him that so they fucked in the missionary position. He made her cum. He came all over her. He left.

Another time, she was in bed with him. As he was getting ready to enter her, she said, 'I'm such a whore for you.' He didn't reply, so she said, 'I'm a whore and a slut.' He still didn't respond. She probably should have let it go but she asked him, 'What do you think I am?'

He said, 'I think you're a beautiful, sexy woman.'

'You don't think I'm a whore and a slut?'

He smiled and said, 'Not my scene.'

He didn't even want her to vary the color of the stockings. She asked him if he'd like to see her in black or red ones sometime. He said, 'You look great in the white ones.'

She couldn't interest him in trying anything different.

Chapter Three

~

'Y‍OU SEE WHAT I mean?' said Tina, as she drained another glass of wine.

'Definitely,' said Emma. 'However much you love vanilla ice cream, sometimes you want chocolate sprinkles.'

'It's not like I want anything too bizarre. I don't expect him to have a fully equipped dungeon. But some variation—or deviation—once in a while would be nice.'

'So Kieran's not as good as Steve?' asked Ben.

'Not even close. The trouble is Kieran's always so nice about everything that I can't get mad at him. It might have been different if he'd been the first. Then, just being with a man who wasn't my husband would have been a big enough turn on. But when you've been there and done that, you start to crave something different. If I could graft his cock onto a guy with a few twists and turns in his mind, I'd be more than happy. With Steve, I never knew what was going to happen next. Sure, some of the things shouldn't have happened. That's another piece of advice, by the way. Don't let anyone take photos of you.'

'Does that include me?' asked Ben.

Tina didn't answer him. She seemed miles away, her

expression dreamy and nostalgic. 'It was like Steve had studied the blueprints of my body. He always touched me in the right place, in the right way, at the right time. He knew when to go fast, when to go slow, when to wait. That's worth more than a huge cock. Compared to Kieran, Steve was fun size. It wasn't much bigger than yours, was it, babe?'

I thought she was sharing too much. There were people I'd known for twenty years who had no idea about the size of my cock. I picked up the bottle of wine and poured a little into my own glass. Then I put the bottle down, out of Tina's reach.

'Why did you stop seeing him?' asked Ben.

Tina's face hardened. 'He fell in love with me. He wanted all or nothing. Guess which one he got.'

'He went psycho on you?' asked Emma.

She shuddered. 'They say hell hath no fury like a woman scorned. If you want real fury, tell an arrogant stud you don't want to fuck him anymore. He tried to blackmail us. I could have lost my job. Oh yes, that's another thing. Don't go with anyone from work.'

Emma shrugged. 'I don't work.'

'Could you pass the wine?' said Tina to Ben. He gave me an apologetic look and handed it to her. She filled her glass and Emma's. 'Where are you thinking of looking?'

'I've already found someone.'

'Really? I thought this was still in the planning stages.'

'It is. We haven't done anything yet—well, hardly anything. But I know who it's going to be. He's called Mark.'

'Where did you meet him?'

'He's Ben's best friend.'

Tina shook her head vigorously. 'No, no, no!'

'What?'

'That has trouble written all over it.'

'What do you mean?'

She turned to Ben. 'Do your families know each other?'

'Oh yes,' he said. 'His dad works for mine.'

'I don't like this at all. Imagine if your family found out.'

'I don't think Mark tells his dad all the details of his sex life,' said Ben with a wry smile.

'I didn't think Steve would threaten to tell our boss.'

'I hear what you're saying,' said Emma. 'But ….' She reached into her bag and took out her phone. She pressed a couple of buttons and showed her phone to Tina. 'That's Mark.'

Tina looked at the screen. 'Okay, I see what you mean.'

'Swipe left to see him on the beach.'

Tina swiped left and her eyes widened. 'Fuck, yeah!'

Emma leaned back and crossed her arms, looking a little smug. 'I think he's worth taking a few risks for. Don't you?'

'I would sell the family silver for five minutes alone with him,' admitted Tina.

I was glad we didn't have any silver.

Tina handed me the phone. 'What do you think, babe?'

I saw a man who had just been swimming. The dark brown hair on his head was slicked black and glistening in the sun. He had the burly look of a power lifter rather than the toned definition of a body builder. His chest and arms were big but he looked like he enjoyed his food. He had thick dark hair covering his chest and reaching up to his neck. An arrow of hair pointed from his navel down to his crotch. 'He looks all right,' I said, grudgingly, and handed the phone back to her.

'All right? He's gorgeous.' She turned to Emma again. 'Be careful, hon. Make sure he knows unspeakably nasty things will happen to him if he breathes a word to anyone.'

'Will do.'

Tina took another look at the picture on the phone. 'When you say "hardly anything" …?'

'We've had some fun,' said Emma with a little smile.

Tina topped up Emma's glass. 'Go on.'

'Well, when I got together with Ben, I soon realized he wasn't going to be a run of the mill boyfriend. I went out with a lot of boys before him and they were all so possessive. They started sulking if I so much as looked at another guy. Ben was the opposite. He encouraged me to have roving eyes. I found that out on our first date. He took me to a lovely Italian restaurant. After a few glasses of Barolo, he asked me if I thought our waiter was handsome. My first thought was, "Oh great, he fancies the waiter. Our first date and he comes out." Then he said, "Which men in here do you like?" At the time, I didn't know what he was doing. But I'd had a few glasses as well. It was a more interesting first date question than, "What music are you into?" I spent an enjoyable evening looking round the room, checking out the men. Some of their wives and girlfriends weren't happy—particularly if the guys started looking back. But I enjoyed the effect it had on Ben. He could hardly control himself when I said, "That one over there is amazing." He asked me, "Is he better looking than me?" I could tell he'd be gutted if I said no, so I told him, "Oh, he is so much better than you in every way." Ben let out a moan. I thought he'd cum. After we finished eating, he asked if I wanted to come back to his place for a nightcap. I said no, I was going home to think about all those other men.'

'That's when I knew I was in love,' said Ben.

'When we started seeing each other regularly, we talked so much about other guys that I had a few more doubts. I was waiting for him to stand up and shout, "I can no longer live a lie—I want all these men for myself!" '

'But I didn't,' said Ben. 'In our fantasies, it was always *you* who ended up in bed with the hot studs.'

'Sounds familiar, doesn't it, babe?' said Tina, touching my shoulder. I nodded. 'I invented all these men—and even a woman—I was seeing on the side to keep Rob happy.'

'We didn't invent people,' said Emma. 'They were all real. We saw them in the street, on the train, in shops. I doubt if any of them noticed us. One popped into our local café for a latte to go. He had no idea that he spent the rest of the night taking me roughly from behind.' Emma's eyes gleamed as she said, 'Then

Ben started telling me about his friend, Mark. The amazing Mark. Best-looking boy in his school. Captain of the football team. Guitarist in the local rock band. Ben showed me some photos and asked what I thought of him. And … well, you've seen him. Pretty soon, he became the principal player in our fantasies. As you can imagine, I was keen to meet him. When I did … oh, Tina … he's even better looking when you see him in real life.'

'When *can* I?' asked Tina, innocently.

'We started spending time with him. Nothing strange about that. Ben hanging out with his girlfriend and his best friend. But it was odd, talking about him doing rude things to me half the night and then trying to act normal around him the next day.'

Tina took some deep breaths, which is what she does when she's trying to sober up. 'Do be careful, guys. I can see why you want to do it. But there's a huge difference between fantasy and reality.'

'We know.'

She held up a warning finger. 'We thought we knew, but it was still a shock how different it was. You can control fantasies. You decide how far they go. You decide when they finish.'

'It's may be a bit late to think about that,' said Emma. She thought for a moment. 'I felt like I was in control the whole time. I'm pretty sure I can manage this okay. Because this one time, we went round to see Mark at his place. He was wearing a blue t-shirt and his chest hairs were curling out of the collar. I was hooked. If you'd asked me to make a list of the things I find attractive in a man, I wouldn't have included a hairy chest. But when I saw him, I could feel my heart beating faster. I know we're supposed to go for kindhearted men with a sense of humor—'

'And we've got them,' said Tina, smiling at Ben and me.

'But there are times when I want a big, strong, hairy guy to throw me down on the bed, screw me senseless, and then fuck off.'

'Tell me about it,' said Tina in a low voice. She was breathing heavily and took a big gulp of wine to calm herself down.

The atmosphere in the room was becoming highly charged. I could tell that Tina was thinking about a big, strong, hairy guy screwing *her* senseless. That image and her excitement made my cock hard. I caught Ben's eye. He was shaking a little, obviously turned on by what Emma was saying. He and I raised our glasses—one cuckold to another.

Emma continued, 'I told Ben I was out of cigarettes and asked him to run and get me more. As soon as Mark and I were alone, he said, "You can't stop staring, can you?" He didn't wait for a reply. He took his t-shirt off. I went up to him and told him to part his knees. Maybe he thought his luck was in, but I just knelt between them and ran my hands over his chest. Touching it set off something primitive inside me. I was imagining how it would feel against my boobs. I wondered if I could take my shirt off and rub myself against him there and then. But then I heard Ben coming in. I told Mark to put his t-shirt back on. I sat down and picked up my cup of tea.'

'They were sitting there, looking all innocent,' said Ben, trying to speak calmly. 'But the air was humming.' He looked at Emma with lust in his eyes. 'You were like a couple of feral dogs.'

She ruffled his hair. 'I didn't think you were ready to see me in full flow with your best friend.'

'I was *so* ready. It would have been incredible to walk in and find you rubbing your breasts against him.'

My first thought was that if Ben wanted to see Emma with her tits on another man's chest, I'd be happy to volunteer. But that wasn't my role in this story. I looked at Tina. Would I like to see her with one of my friends? I didn't think so. My emotions when she was cucking me were complicated enough, without throwing betrayal of friendship into the mix. I couldn't see this ending well for Ben. There was a real chance he'd lose both his girlfriend and his best friend. But Emma had set her sights on Mark. And she looked like a girl who was used to getting what she wanted.

'Why do you want Emma to go with another man so much?' asked Tina.

'Well—' he began.

There was a small, cruel smile on Emma's face. 'Rather than explaining, why don't you show her?'

'I don't think—'

She spoke to him with a sudden sharpness. 'Show Goddess Tina why you need someone else to satisfy me.'

Tina raised her eyebrows. She'd never been called "Goddess" before. But she wasn't complaining. Ben still hesitated. 'You don't want me to get cross, do you, Ben?' said Emma, still in that stern, teacher's voice.

Ben stood up, unbuckled his belt and lowered his trousers and shorts. 'Guys,' I said, 'we've all had a lot to drink and maybe we're going too far here.'

Tina put her hand on my arm. 'It's their thing, babe. Let them do it.'

Chapter Four

~

I HAD TO FEEL sorry for Ben. His cock was less than an inch long. Emma pushed his pubes out of the way so we could see it properly. He was blushing hotly. As we watched, his cock did start to harden and push itself forwards. Fully erect, it might have been two and a half inches. 'What do you think?' asked Emma.

'It's quite small,' said Tina.

'*Quite* small?' echoed Emma. 'It's *tiny*. Is it the smallest you've ever seen?'

'Probably. Kieran's is at least four times that size. Even Rob's is a lot bigger. Rob, why don't you—?'

'No,' I said firmly.

Fortunately, Tina didn't pursue that idea.

'What did I say the first time I saw it?' Emma asked Ben.

'You kept on repeating, "Is that all you've got?" '

'You remember what else I did?'

'You cried a little.'

'Imagine how I felt. I'd met the person I wanted to spend the rest of my life with. He was kind, generous, and clearly adored me. Then we went to bed and I saw this. It's more of a clit than a prick. I feel like a lesbian with that in my mouth.'

'You put *that* in your mouth?' asked Tina.

She rolled her eyes. 'I know. The things we do for love. I suppose I should have expected it. After all, why else would he be obsessed with picturing me and other men?'

'Not necessarily,' said Tina. 'Rob's totally obsessed and, like I was saying, his cock's pretty big. His problem is—'

'So, Ben, do *you* work?' I asked. I knew it was a strange question to ask a man with his cock out, but I was desperate to change the subject.

'Yes,' he replied, 'my father owns a large car distribution company. He's taken me on as—'

Tina was not going to be put off. 'Rob's problem is he cums too quickly. After he's been inside me for thirty seconds, he screws his face up and I know he's trying not to shoot his load.'

Part of me badly wanted Tina to shut up. But my cock—damn him—was getting hard again.

'At least you know when he's inside you,' said Emma.

'Did you let Ben fuck you that first time?' asked Tina.

Emma sighed. 'Yes, I did. It was like going to the new *Transformers* film. You think it can't possibly be as bad as it looks.'

'But it was?'

'He tried going in at different angles. We tried a number of positions. I couldn't feel anything. Fortunately, he has a few toys and a lot of batteries. Ultimately, I was satisfied, but not in the way I wanted to be.'

'I know what you mean. Rob's an absolute master at cunnilingus, but it's not the same as—'

'Err … ladies,' I said, indicating Ben.

'Oh, yes,' said Emma. 'Ben, apologize to Goddess Tina for the size of your prick.'

'I'm sorry for the size of my prick, Goddess Tina,' said Ben.

Tina shrugged, as if the size of Ben's prick hadn't inconvenienced her all that much.

'You can put it away now.' He covered himself up and sat down. Emma stood up and took her bag from the back of her chair. 'I need to go out to your garden for a minute. I'm trying to cut down. But I still like one after dinner.'

'I'll come with you,' said Tina.

'Do you smoke?'

'No, but I'll keep you company. And the dog might want to pee. Come on, Boris.'

Tina and Emma went out. Boris trotted behind them. Ben and I were left at the table. 'Are you okay?' I asked him.

He chuckled. 'I'm fine. Believe it or not, Emma does love me.'

'Oh, I do believe it. She seems rather brutal with you, though.'

'Tina can be harsh too.'

'Tina likes teasing. With Emma, it's more like humiliation. At least I could say no.'

'If I'd really wanted to, I could have said no too. But the chance to have two women teasing me about my cock—I'm not going to pass that one up. And—I hope you don't mind me saying this—Tina's sexy.'

I smiled. 'I'm used to other men finding my wife attractive.'

'I'm jealous of you, serving a woman like that.'

'I don't *serve* her. There is a hard side to her, which we both like. But there's no mistress and slave stuff here.'

He raised an apologetic hand. 'I didn't mean—'

'Don't worry. It can't be easy for people to understand what's going on with Tina and me. The truth is, most of the time we're like any other married couple.'

'Are you?'

I leaned back in my chair. 'Yes. It's a bit like … well, a teacher at the language school where I work is gay. He gets annoyed when people expect him to do "gay" things all the time. They're surprised when he says he's looking forward to the new *Star Wars* film—like he's not allowed to watch anything except *Brokeback Mountain*. They assume he listens to Liza Minnelli all the time and act like he's joking when he says he likes Bryan Adams. It's the same with being a cuckold. Tina and I aren't constantly doing "cuckoldy" things. We have toast and coffee in the morning. We eat pizza and watch crime dramas in the evening. We talk about trips we want to take and we fret over our mortgage repayments. If I've got a problem, Tina's the first person I go to. She's the same with me. Ninety-nine percent— well, maybe ninety percent of the time—we're like anyone else. We just have this extra aspect to our relationship. And that's the way I like it. Because when the alarm goes off on Monday morning, I don't want to kiss my mistress's boots. I want to eat breakfast and go to work.'

He nodded. Then he asked, 'If you could be like any other couple *all* the time, if you could press a button and put things back to the way they were before she met this … Steve, is it?'

'That's right.'

'Would you?'

I was silent for a moment as I pondered his question. 'I've often thought about that. There are times when I want Tina all to myself again. But … I don't think I could go back.'

'Why not?'

'Because the ten percent of my life that's about being a cuckold has great highs and great lows. When you watch Emma undressing in front of Mark for the first time, you will *feel* so much. You'll be more turned on than ever before. You'll also be jealous, angry, proud and protective—all at the same time. Every nerve in your body will be electrified. It won't be comfortable but you'll sure know you're alive. Then, afterwards, you'll hate both of them for betraying you. But not as much as you'll hate yourself for letting it happen. You'll be disgusted, but you'll still know you're alive.' I paused, remembering.

I shook myself out of it and continued, 'Now, compare that with how most "normal" people feel. They spend the day at work and … it's all right. It's not great. It's not terrible. It's just what they do. When they're not working, they watch TV, they go shopping, they have a beer. And … it's all right. It's what most of my life is like, too. But if Tina told me tomorrow she was going to stop cuckolding me, *all* my life would be just that—all right. I'm not sure I can go back to that.'

He nodded. 'I see what you mean.'

'Do you love Emma?'

His sigh was deep and soulful. 'Totally. Completely.'

'Because, more than anything else, a cuckold relationship is about love. If you don't love her, you're just watching two people have sex. You might as well see a porn show.'

'If she goes with Mark, I'll love both of them.'

'Not an experience I've ever had. But I agree with Tina on that one. Do be careful.' I leaned forward to give my words extra emphasis. 'You're putting yourself into a situation where passions run high. Emma was talking about Mark unleashing something primitive inside her. Well, he might get a bit primitive as well. Two men, both attracted to one woman. In the history of humankind, nothing has caused more fights than that.'

Ben was unconvinced. 'He's my oldest friend,' he said, spreading his arms.

I gave him my best give-me-a-break look. 'And old friends have never fallen out over a girl.'

'One thing Mark liked to do when we were kids was smash my toys. The first time he did, I screamed and told my mom. But after a while, I realized I was leaving my toys in his way just so he'd smash them. It's an unusual friendship. He takes whatever he wants and I let him. It's always been like that.'

'And you like it?' It was my turn to be surprised.

He nodded. 'You think I'm strange?'

I shook my head. 'I watch my wife getting fucked by other men. I'm in no position to judge anyone.'

'What advice would *you* give *me*?'

'Always show Emma that you love her. However much she says she wants to do this, there'll be part of her that's thinking,

"If he really loved me, he wouldn't share me with anyone else." So you've got to be extra attentive.'

He nodded again. 'Got you.'

Tina and Emma came back in. 'I didn't realize how late it was,' said Emma. 'We'd better make a move, Ben.' Emma kissed Tina and me on the cheek. Ben shook my hand. 'It's been so good to meet you both,' said Emma.

'Great to meet you too,' said Tina. 'I hope some of the things I said made sense.'

'It's been useful. See you soon.'

We showed them out and stood in the doorway waving as they drove off.

'Interesting evening,' I said, closing the door.

'Yes,' agreed Tina. 'I've never been to a dinner party where a guest got his cock out.'

'We obviously go to the wrong dinner parties.'

She gave me a pointed look. 'And you can stop drooling now, babe.'

'What do you mean?'

'You know what I mean. You couldn't keep your eyes off Emma.'

'I hardly noticed her.'

'Oh please. You were gazing at her like she was the Taj Mahal by moonlight. You think she's beautiful?'

I shrugged. 'She's all right, if you like that sort of thing.'

'What—young, pretty, and sexy?'

'That's not what I meant.'

'You don't like young, pretty, and sexy women? So why are you with me?'

'There's no way I can get out of this, is there?'

'No.' We went back into the dining room and sat down. She poured the last of the wine into our glasses. 'What did you think of Ben?'

'He's nice. Emma's got him where she wants him.'

'Firmly under her thumb.'

'Exactly. Do you want me to call you "Goddess" now?'

She laughed. 'Can't do any harm.'

'And do you want me to apologize for my cock?'

'Not the size. Mind you, I'm starting to wish you did have a tiny cock. I could have a lot of fun teasing you about it. Can you get cock reduction surgery?'

'Least popular operation ever.'

'For the moment, you'll have to stick with apologizing for never making me cum when you're fucking me.'

'I *am* sorry for that,' I said in all sincerity.

Tina gave me her cruelest look. 'I should have made you fuck me in front of them. You'd have lasted ten seconds. It would have been delicious to hear Emma laughing at you.' She felt the bulge in my trousers. 'Someone likes that idea.' She unzipped my trousers, reached in and pulled out my cock. She held it in her hand and pushed her nails into the tender skin. I winced. 'You could never satisfy a girl like Emma. Anyway, she's way out of your league. She wouldn't even give you a pity fuck.'

I was breathing heavily. My arousal was only intensified by the pain in my cock. 'Do you think that Mark guy would satisfy you?' I asked.

'Oh yes. He can satisfy me any time he wants.'

'You want me to pretend to be him tonight?'

'You know I do. And I want you to fuck me from behind.'

'Why?'

She released my cock and undid a couple of buttons on my shirt. She reached her hand in, rubbed my chest and made a face. 'Because I don't want to feel your hairless chest on my tits.'

She went upstairs. I told her I'd be up in a minute. I had an idea, but I wasn't sure if it would work. I went to the closet under the stairs. Tina had a black fur coat—fake fur, of course—with a detachable hood. I took the hood upstairs and opened the bedroom door. The room was in darkness, but I could see by the landing light that she was naked on the bed on all fours. I went into the room and closed the door behind me. 'Is that you, Mark?' she asked.

'Sure is,' I said in a low, gruff voice. I had no idea how Mark spoke, but neither did she, so talking wouldn't spoil the illusion. I knelt on the bed behind her. 'Emma tells me you've got a thing for hairy men.'

I held the furry hood up to my chest and stroked it against her ass. 'Feel my hairy chest.'

She moaned. 'That's a real man's body. I bet you've got a real man's cock, as well.'

I opened the bedside table drawer and took out a box of condoms. I made some noise opening the box and taking a condom out. But I didn't put it on. I was hoping she wouldn't notice that I'd also taken out one of her vibrators. It was eight inches long and covered with soft pink rubber. She always said it was the one that felt most like a real cock. I didn't turn it on. I pushed it into her cunt and moved it in and out. Every time it was fully inside her, I touched the hood against her ass.

'What the …? Oh, *yes*.' She wasn't sure what I was doing, but she was enjoying it. I thrust the vibrator into her, slow and deep. After ten minutes, she was moaning and panting. 'Am I better than Emma?' she asked.

I was fairly sure Mark had never fucked Emma. But this wasn't the time to point that out. I had a quick decision to make. Was she looking for compliments or teasing?

'Emma's history,' I said. 'She's nothing compared to you. I'm going to forget about Emma and satisfy a real woman.'

I'd made the right choice. Tina pushed back against the vibrator, getting it even more deeply inside her. I felt the muscles of her cunt grip it tightly and she came with a long deep groan. She took an extra moment to enjoy the feel of it inside her. Pulling it out of her, I stashed it and the hood under the bed.

Afterwards, she lay with her head on me. She seemed to have forgotten how much she hated my hairless chest. 'What did you do there?' she asked.

I felt like a magician; I didn't want to give away how the trick was done. 'The hood from your black coat.'

She giggled. 'Clever.'

'I felt a bit silly, doing it.'

'It's what every girl dreams of—being rubbed down with synthetic fibers.'

'It was probably too soft.'

'Yes. A man's chest hair is springier and wirier. But it did the job. It helped me to imagine Mark.'

'You've never been into hairy chests before.'

'No, I suppose not. Like Emma, I wouldn't have put it on my list of attractive qualities. When you made me watch those old James Bond movies, I didn't get too turned on when Sean Connery took his shirt off.'

'And you remember that bar we went to where all the men were dressed as cops and firemen? The guy you picked up there was hairy. You liked it but it wasn't that important to you.'

There was something diabolical about Tina's chuckle. 'Maybe Mark will be the one to change my mind.'

'He's all set to be Emma's stud.'

She lifted her head. Even in the dark room, I could see the sparkle of her teeth. She was giving me her grin. 'Have you ever known me to want a man and not get him?'

Chapter Five

~

THE NEXT MORNING, I woke up at ten, still tired and my head felt heavy. The bed beside me was empty, so I put on my robe and went downstairs. When Boris came up to say good morning, I knelt down to pat him and he licked my face. We went to find Tina.

She was sitting at the dining room table, looking at something on her laptop. I put my arms around her and kissed her neck.

'Morning, babe,' she said, kissing my cheek. 'How are you?'

'I'm not feeling great today.' I picked up one of the empty bottles from the table and looked at it sadly. 'I might have to face the fact that me and red wine are through.'

'That's a shame. You've had good times together.'

'I know, but I'm not the same person anymore.'

'Do you mind if I still see old red from time to time? We've gotten quite close over the last few months.'

'I noticed. You seemed on very good terms last night. You been up long?'

'Over an hour. I took Boris for a run in the park and gave him breakfast. You were dead to the world so I didn't want to wake you.'

'Thanks. What are you doing now?'

She pointed to the laptop. She was on cuckoldchat.com, talking to someone who called himself curiousgeorge. 'I don't think he's going to be the next stud to rock my world,' she said. I looked at the screen.

curiousgeorge: *what are you wearing?*

Tina thought for a second, then typed,

hotwife37: *black stockings, suspenders, bra and pants*

She was wearing an old t-shirt with a picture of Betty Boop on it. 'Should you mention those pants are on fire?' I asked her.

She shrugged. 'He's alone on a Saturday morning. Let's brighten up his weekend.'

curiousgeorge: *any pix?*

She sighed and muttered, 'Oh, here we go.'

hotwife37: *Yes, I have a complete portfolio of sexy pictures and I can't wait to share them with some random dude. It's literally all I want to do.*

GoddessE has entered the chat room.

GoddessE: *Hi Tina!*

'It's Emma,' said Tina.

curiousgeorge: *Great. Send me one of you bending over in just your black pants.*

Tina closed curiousgeorge's window with a contemptuous click of the mouse. 'I'm not chatting to anyone who doesn't appreciate irony.' She clicked on GoddessE's window.

hotwife37: *Hey, Emma. How are you?*

GoddessE: *Mortified.*

hotwife37: *Why?*

GoddessE: *I can't believe the things I did last night. The wine went straight to my head.*

hotwife37: *You didn't do anything wrong, hon.*

GoddessE: *I show up at your place, I get drunk, I ask you a whole lot of personal questions and I make my boyfriend show you his prick.*

hotwife37: *After all the things we'd chatted about in here, I wasn't too surprised.*

GoddessE: *You don't hate me?*

hotwife37: *Of course not.*

GoddessE: *Good. Because it was great to meet you. Rob's a nice guy.*

'You've got a fan, babe,' said Tina.

hotwife37: *Yes, he is.*

GoddessE: *Are you sure he's your cuck? He looks like he could be a pretty fine stud.*

'Listen to your friend,' I said, allowing myself a few seconds to imagine life as Emma's stud.

'Sorry to burst your bubble, babe, but ....'

hotwife37: *He could give you the best twenty seconds of your life.*

GoddessE: *lol*

'I don't know if it's laugh out loud funny,' I said, coming back to earth. 'Quiet smile, maybe.'

hotwife37: *Ben's a nice guy, too. Crazy for you.*

GoddessE: *True. Shame he doesn't measure up in some areas.*

hotwife37: *I noticed. But he seems happy for you to look elsewhere.*

GoddessE: *On that subject ... We're going round to Mark's place today. I think it's time to stop messing about and tell him what I want.*

hotwife37: *Are you sure he's the right one?*

GoddessE: *You saw him!!!!*

hotwife37: *He's Ben's friend.*

GoddessE: *That just adds extra spice to it!*

hotwife37: *Why don't you go to a bar and pick up a stranger?*

GoddessE: *Because I want Mark.*

hotwife37: *Or there are studs who advertise on this site.*

GoddessE: *And none of them come close to Mark. Got to go. Talk to you later. Have a great day!*

GoddessE has left the room.

'She won't listen,' said Tina, as she logged out of the site and switched off the laptop. 'I don't want her and Ben to get hurt.'

'That's your only reason for trying to steer her away from Mark?' I asked.

'Of course. What other reason could there be?'

Chapter Six

~

EVER SINCE TINA HAD told me about Steve making her a full Cordon Bleu style meal, I'd been trying to make my cooking more adventurous. On Friday evening, I made a soufflé, which I served with tomato salad. I brought the plates into the den where Tina was sitting. She prodded the soufflé suspiciously with her fork. Then she took a bite and made a face. 'It's blue cheese.'

'You like blue cheese,' I reminded her.

'I do, but it gives me horrible breath.'

'I'll still kiss you.'

'What about anyone else?'

'Do you have another man hiding under the couch?' I checked, just in case.

She gave me a playful slap and waggled her eyebrows. 'You never can tell with me.'

'What's happened so far?' I asked, pointing at the television.

'A woman went into her apartment and surprised an intruder. She seemed to know him and was on the point of saying a name. Now she's in a chair, bound and gagged. I do not—'

I joined in. 'I do not have high hopes for her future.' I poured us each a glass of red wine.

'I thought you and red were finished,' she said.

'We were. But at the end of the soufflé recipe, it says, "Serve with a robust red wine." Orders are orders.'

We finished our dinner and put the plates on the floor. Boris eyed the residue but was too well behaved to lick them without permission. Instead, he saw his cue to jump up and stretch himself across our laps. Tina patted his head and whispered in his ear, 'Don't hate me, honey, but you'll have to get down in a second.'

'You need to go pee?' I asked.

She shook her head. 'How much wine have you had?'

'A couple of sips.'

'Are you okay to drive?'

'I guess so. Why?'

'I'm not in the mood for a quiet evening in. I want to go out and have a few drinks. Maybe dance. And … there's a new bar that's opened up a few miles out of town—especially for people like us.'

'Dog lovers, you mean? People who watch crime dramas?'

'Yes. It's full of people in *NCIS* t-shirts passing round pictures of spaniels. There may also be some hot wives there with their cucks, and if we're lucky, one or two hunky studs. A couple of women on the site were talking about this place.'

I didn't really want to go out. 'I thought you were after Mark.'

'I am. But I want to get some practice in first.'

'No chance you'll settle for me?'

'Sorry, babe. I'm in the mood for an epic, not a two-minute short.'

She pointed at the floor. Boris grumbled but jumped down. She went upstairs to change, but I took the dishes into the kitchen. I didn't see any reason why I should change, since I was fairly sure no one would be looking at me. I tickled Boris behind his ear and told him, 'You're going to get some me-time, buddy. I don't know when we'll be back. We might even have a new friend with us. You make sure and scare him away if he tries to stay the night.'

Tina came back down. She looked sexy in skintight purple trousers with black boots. She was also wearing a black leather jacket with a low-cut black t-shirt. Her hair was spiked up into her trademark porcupine spines, and she smelled of mouthwash. 'Let's go!'

She'd printed off the map from the bar's website and gave me directions from the passenger seat. We got lost a couple of times, but we finally arrived. There was a wooden sign on the front of the building that said THE MEETING PLACE in big red letters. It looked like any other bar, except that drapes were drawn across all the windows.

A large bald man in a black suit was standing outside. 'Good evening, madam. Good evening, sir. May I ask how you found out about this establishment?'

'A recommendation on cuckoldchat.com,' said Tina.

That was good enough for him. He nodded and opened the door. 'Have fun,' he said.

We went inside, happy to discover it wasn't too brightly lit. Tony Bennett was crooning quietly in the background. Some people were on the dance floor. Most were sitting around talking. Once we found a table, I went to the bar and bought a white wine for Tina and a Coke for me.

'What do you think of this place?' asked Tina, when I got back to our table.

'It's all right,' I said. 'At least you can hear yourself think.'

She rolled her eyes. 'That's such an old man thing to say. "Why does the music have to be so loud?" '

I laughed and played along. 'In our day, the songs had tunes!'

'This is still our day, babe,' she said. 'But I agree with you. I hate places that are too loud. Now, do you see any men?'

'Plenty. Most of them are here with their wives and girlfriends, though.'

'I know. Unless a few studs show up, this might turn into a cuck-swapping party.'

I widened my eyes in exaggerated excitement. 'Does that mean I get to have sex with all these women?'

'Yeah, right. I'm not swapping you, babe.' She kissed me on the forehead. 'What about that guy at the bar? He looks like he's on his own.'

'Possibly. Why, do you like the look of him?'

'He'd do in a pinch. I'm not sure I'd go all the way. But if he wanted to lick my pussy, I wouldn't complain.'

'And would you return the compliment?'

She gave me a nudge. 'It would only be polite.'

'Do you think he's got anything worth sucking?'

'There's a bulge in those jeans. A good mouthful, at least.'

We were both looking over at the bar, so it took us a few minutes to realize that a man was standing in front of our table, smiling at us. 'Good evening, my name's Adam,' he said. 'Do you mind if I join you for a while?' He was a handsome man in his late forties, maybe even early fifties. His hair had once been brown but now was mostly gray. He had a well-trimmed salt-and-pepper beard. His eyes were a striking gray-blue and there was a playful twist to his mouth.

Tina had never gone for the George Clooney look. I could see the beginnings of her *sorry, this isn't going to happen* smile. He held up his hand. 'Don't worry. I have no interest in having sex with you. May I?'

He sat down, picked up Tina's glass and sniffed it. 'Chardonnay,' he said. He looked over and caught the barman's eye. 'A bottle of the Chardonnay and three glasses over here, please.'

I would have expected any barman to answer with a curt 'Order at the bar like everyone else,' but this one gave Adam a thumbs-up, and a minute later, we had a bottle on the table.

Adam poured us all a drink. 'To love—in its many forms,' he said. Before we could respond, he carried on, 'I've been watching the couples in here. Most of them are finished. This is their last attempt to resuscitate a marriage that's already dead.' He pointed discreetly to a couple two tables away. 'They'll be calling their lawyers in the morning whether she gets fucked tonight or not. You see the way he's stabbing the crushed ice in his mojito with a straw? It's like he hates ice and wants it to die. The truth is, he hates his life and blames the woman sitting next to him. He's got a pretty good job. He can afford a smart suit. He drinks cocktails instead of beer to show what a classy guy he is. But he's trapped. They've got a couple of children and a huge mortgage. He knows he can't show his ass to his boss and go off to follow his dream. Now look at *her*. She keeps playing with her hair because she's worried it's not cascading down her shoulders in quite the perfect way. She has slathered on lipstick and eyeliner, which makes her look like the lovechild of Mick Jagger and Bambi. Before they came here, she told him, "Hey, I've got a great idea—it'll be smoking hot if I go with another guy, but don't worry, sweetie, I'll always be in love with you." The truth is, she's looking for her prince. The good-looking, funny man she married is tired and stressed all the time now. He works a twelve-hour day. When he comes home, the only thing he wants to do is sit down with his dinner and watch TV. They haven't had sex in three months. She's decided she deserves better. What she wants is a guy to take her off to a magical kingdom where people are rich without working all the time. She kids herself she's going to find someone like that here.'

He indicated another couple sitting on the opposite side of the room. 'And you see those two? Do you notice *he's* the one scanning the room, looking for men? Occasionally, he points one out to her. But her lips are pursed. Her arms are folded. Her reaction to every man is the same—a brief shake of the head. She doesn't want to be here. This was his idea. He reckons a thriving sex life is the key to a happy marriage. So to fix their relationship, he's suggested everything—dressing up, roleplay,

S&M. This is his last throw of the dice—except he doesn't know that. She's disgusted with him. She's asking herself why she married this pervert and wondering how much money she needs to get out of this marriage and start over on her own.'

'You got all that just by looking at them?' I asked.

'You can tell a lot from watching people,' he said with a smile. 'That's why I wanted to talk to you two.'

'You've been watching us?'

'Ever since you came in. If I had to guess, I'd say you were called Robert.'

'How the—?' I began.

'Your wallet has the letters RPM stamped into the leather. Now, that could mean you're a vinyl junkie. But I'm going to assume those are your initials. The most popular man's name beginning with R is Robert. So … Robert Paul Martin?'

'Robert Patrick Matthews.'

He smiled again. 'No method is foolproof.'

'What's my name?' asked Tina.

He looked her over. 'You're going to have to give me a clue.'

'T.'

'Teresa, Tammy, Tina, Tracy, Tiffany.'

'Third time lucky.'

'Tina.'

'That's right. Are you a psychiatrist or something?'

He smiled quietly. 'Something.'

'What else do you know about us?' she asked. She may not have found him attractive, but she was certainly curious about him. I have to say I was too.

'When you went off to the bar, Robert—'

'Rob.'

'Rob. Tina was checking out the guys like she's supposed to but she also kept glancing over at you. When you sat down together, you automatically held hands under the table. Then you realized that wasn't the image you wanted to project in a place like this. When you talk to each other, your heads are almost touching. Each of you wants to hear what the other one is saying. You smile at the same time, laugh at the same time. You're still very much in love, and more than that, you're still best friends. I don't see many couples like you in here. It was probably Tina's idea to come here. But you're excited, Rob. You like the possibility of Tina having sex with another man tonight. You're confident you'll still be Rob and Tina, the happy couple, tomorrow. So what are you looking for tonight? Who would be your ideal?'

She rested her chin on her hand and began, 'Well, it helps if he's good-looking.'

'You want more than that.'

'I suppose I'd like him to be big.'

'When you say big …?'

'In both senses,' she said with a smile.

'Stronger than Rob?'

'I suppose so.'

He put his chin on his hand. 'What else?'

'A hairy chest would be an added bonus.'

He looked at me. 'You don't have a hairy chest?'

'No,' I replied, 'I've evolved beyond that. I don't live in a tree, either.'

He smiled briefly and looked at Tina again. 'This is a recent interest.'

'A friend of mine showed me a picture of a stud she's pursuing. I felt something.'

'Where do you think that came from?'

'What do you mean?'

'Think back to when you were a girl. Do you remember anyone with a hairy chest?'

'I can't think of anyone,' she said, but she looked down and blushed.

'Yes, you can.'

'My best friend when I was a kid was Lucy. It was her birthday one year. Her dad took a whole lot of us to the beach. It was a hot day. I remember he took his shirt off. He had a hairy chest. I'd never seen anything like that before.'

'What do you remember about him on that day?'

'He was brilliant. Fourteen kids on a beach. He didn't have to shout. He didn't bribe us with sweets. He told us what he wanted and we did it.'

'He had charisma.'

'I'd call it natural authority.'

'Do you think you're looking for a man like that?'

She frowned. 'I'm not looking for a dominant person, if that's what you mean. I'm not submissive.'

'That's obvious. You *are* looking for something else, though. After all, you already have Rob and … someone else as well.'

'How did you know that?'

'There's no desperation about you. You're interested in what's on offer. If you find a man tonight, that's great. If you don't, it's not the end of the world. You're a gourmet considering the dessert trolley rather than a starving woman at the all-you-can-eat buffet.'

'Yes, I've got someone else. He's a nice enough guy.'

'Sorry to hear that.'

'Why sorry?'

'Do you think Catherine ever said of Heathcliff, "He's a nice enough guy"? You want your husband to be nice. No problems there, clearly. But it's not what you want from your lover.'

She took a sip of her drink. 'He's not very … imaginative.'

'So you're looking for a man who will take you to interesting places.' Before she could answer, he said, 'I'd better leave you to it. You're not going to meet anyone while I'm here.'

'There's no rush,' said Tina.

'I wouldn't mind staying in touch, though.'

'Do you ever go onto the cuckoldchat.com site?' she asked.

'I will now.'

'Look out for hotwife37.'

'Look out for Adam,' he replied. 'I hope you both find what

you're looking for. Have a good night.' He stood up and walked off.

Tina sat quietly for a while. She was looking into her glass, obviously deep in thought, so I didn't say anything. Eventually she turned to me. 'Shall we go home, babe?'

'Don't you want to find someone?'

She looked around the room. A couple of hot wives were clinging to studs on the dance floor. The cucks were sitting at tables, watching with varying degrees of excitement and jealousy. 'No,' she said, 'let's go home and have a quiet evening with our dog.'

We went out. The bald man at the door looked at us. 'No luck?' he asked.

'No,' said Tina.

'It seems a shame a beautiful woman like you doesn't get what she wants.'

Tina looked him up and down. He was big and strong. I thought for a moment she might be tempted. 'Maybe next time.'

Chapter Seven

~

Goddess*E* has entered the *chat room*

hotwife37: *Hey, Emma. How's it going?*

GoddessE: *Great. U?*

hotwife37: *pretty good—thank you for saving me from the boring men in here*

GoddessE: *you're welcome—well, congratulate me*

hotwife37: *Congratulations! Err … on what?*

GoddessE: *I have officially become a hot girlfriend—if that's the right term*

hotwife37: *It is now. Great! Was it Mark?*

GoddessE: *Yes*

hotwife37: *How was it?*

GoddessE: *Do you want to hear all the gory details?*

Tina paused for a couple of seconds before she typed.

hotwife37: *Yes*

GoddessE: *Why don't you guys come over? There's a pretty good bottle of champagne in the fridge*

'We're not doing anything else today, are we, babe?' Tina asked me.

'No. Are you sure you want to hear about this?'

'Why wouldn't I?'

hotwife37: *Let's have your address. We'll be over ASAP*

We took a taxi so I could drink champagne. Emma answered the door with a glass in her hand. She wasn't drunk, but she was happier and more animated than most people are on a Sunday morning. She gave us a quick tour of the large studio apartment. Sunlight flooded into the living room through the bay windows. The floor was polished wood with a sheepskin rug in the middle. A brown leather couch and two matching armchairs faced a huge television screen set into one wall. The kitchen was all marble work surfaces and spotless white cupboards. It was far too opulent for people their age.

We sat down in the living room, immediately noticing the empty champagne bottle on the coffee table. Ben opened another and poured us all a glass. 'To hot wives and hot girlfriends,' said Emma.

'And to the cucks who love us,' added Tina. We all clinked glasses. 'So, yesterday ….'

Emma settled herself into an armchair and lit a cigarette, while Ben put an ashtray on the floor by her feet.

'Ben phoned Mark yesterday morning and asked if we could go over to his place. But Mark said he was just off to play golf. Ben told him we had something to talk to him about. So Mark said, "Why can't you tell me on the phone?" This threw Ben completely. The poor love was umming and aahing so much, I had to take the phone off him. I said, "Listen, Mark … how's it going?" Then I realized *I* wasn't sure how I was going to put it.'

'We've all been there,' said Tina. She was leaning forward in anticipation, hanging on Emma's every word.

'I wasn't expecting to ask him over the phone. I thought we'd be face to face so I could twirl my hair and flirt. Then I said, "You were at school with Ben. You all showered together after football. Do you really think he could satisfy?" And he said, "Finally! I was wondering when you'd ask." Arrogant sod. Running your fingers over a guy's chest doesn't necessarily mean you want him to screw you. Anyway, I asked him again if we could come over. But he said—get this—"It's got to be at Ben's place. I'll come over after my game." I was pissed off he wouldn't cancel golf for me. He said it would give me time to get ready. He was very specific about what I had to wear.'

'Like Kieran and his white stockings.'

Emma rolled her eyes. 'I wish it were just a pair of stockings he wanted. He told me to wear a black sports-style bra, black hipster panties, black stockings and suspenders with *white* high heels. He also wanted a black necklace and I had to wax— not shave—my armpits. He didn't want even a shadow of hair under my arms.'

'A man who knows what he wants.'

'I don't know why it was so important to him.'

'Men often have very definite ideas,' Tina said. She was handling Emma's story well so far, quite the cuckold philosopher. 'Maybe it's what his ex-girlfriend used to wear. Or it might have been a picture from a formative porn mag. The sports-style bra is a new one on me, though. There could be some athlete he has a thing for.'

'I sent Ben out to buy the clothes while I waxed my armpits.'

'You get some funny looks when you're a man on your own browsing the stockings and suspenders,' said Ben. He had the shell-shocked look I knew only too well. His fantasy had become his reality and he wasn't yet sure how to react.

'When Ben came home, I put the outfit on and sat around,' continued Emma. 'I waited ages. I'm not used to that. When he finally arrived, I said, "How long does it take to play a round of golf?" You know what he said? "We always go for a drink after the game." ' She looked at me. 'Would you sit around in a bar if I were waiting for you?'

'I'd come running,' I said.

'Would you, babe?' asked Tina, giving me a look.

'Well, I would if I weren't married to a beautiful, sexy woman.'

'Nice save.'

Emma carried on, 'Plus, he was wearing jeans and an old t-shirt. After the fuss he'd made about what he wanted me to wear, you'd think he'd have made more of an effort. I was angry with him. But that kind of made me want him more, if you know what I mean.'

'I know exactly what you mean,' said Tina, nodding vigorously.

'Maybe he knew it didn't matter what he wore. He wasn't going to keep it on for long, anyway. As soon as he got in here, he took his t-shirt off, grabbed my wrist and put my hand onto his chest. As I felt the thick hair, it was like something changed inside me. Layers of refinement were stripped away, leaving an animal in heat.' She paused and took a long drag on her cigarette. 'And he hadn't washed. I don't mean he stank or anything. But he had this musky, manly aura around him. That's a better smell than anything from Hugo Boss.'

'Definitely,' said Tina. I wondered if I'd have to stop washing for a couple of days.

'It only works on certain guys,' said Emma. 'If Ben smelled like that, I'd tell him to get under the shower and don't spare the soap.'

'I know. I'd tell Rob the same thing.'

And I had my answer.

'I thought I couldn't be any more turned on,' continued Emma. 'Then he told Ben to draw the curtains. He unbuttoned his jeans and took them down. Oh Tina, I wish you could have seen his prick.'

'So do I,' said Tina. She was certainly seeing it in her mind's eye.

'You've seen Ben's. It's small and pink like a baby mouse. Mark's was like a stick—long and thick and a bit rough. I don't mean it was all veiny. I wouldn't like that. But the skin on Ben's prick is too smooth and soft. Mark's looked like it had seen action. It was surrounded by these thick dark hairs. Standing on the rug over there'—she pointed—'he pushed me down to my knees. I put my lips around his prick. I was careful not to suck too hard. I did not want him finishing in my mouth before he'd had the chance to put it anywhere else. Then he told me to stand up and he took me into the bedroom. He asked Ben very particularly, "This is your bedroom—where you sleep?" He grabbed the black bra we'd bought specially, gave it a wrench and it ripped down the middle.'

Tina made a high-pitched sound in the back of her throat. The more she heard about this Mark guy, the more she liked him. She took a gulp of champagne.

'That's how he saw my boobs for the first time. I stood there, arching my back and pushing my chest forward. Ben's always telling me my body's perfect, the most beautiful in the world. What do you think Mark said? "They're small." "Do you like them?" I said. He shrugged and replied, "I prefer them bigger." '

A little snort of laughter from Tina. 'Smooth talker.' I saw her take a quick look down at her own breasts. I think she was wondering if they'd be big enough for Mark.

'Yeah, right? I wanted to hit him, but not as much as I wanted him to screw me. He told me to take off the panties. I don't know if I'm glad or disappointed he didn't rip them off. He stood in front of me and put a finger into my cunt. Looking me in the eyes, he said, "You're soaking, you dirty little bitch. What do you want?" I replied, "I want you to screw me, you bastard." With a sneer of triumph, he laid me down on the bed. It was Ben who reminded him to put on a condom. Thank heavens he did. I was so out of it, I don't know if I'd have remembered. He didn't mess around. He got on top of me and put his prick inside me. I'd had nothing but Ben's microprick for the last few months, so Mark's came as a shock. But what a great shock. It felt so good to have something I could actually feel inside me. He didn't give me any time to get used to it. He started thrusting immediately. I hadn't expected him to be gentle and he wasn't. He hammered into me as hard as he could. It was like he was trying to hurt me. At that moment, I didn't care. I looked into his face and all I saw was anger. I didn't know what he had to be angry about, but I didn't care about that, either. I was getting the screw I needed. And that gorgeous hairy chest was rubbing against my boobs. My nipples were tingling. Maybe he reckoned I was enjoying it too much, because he turned me over and had me on all fours.

'He took hold of my hips and drove his prick into me from behind. I could feel myself cumming. I'm sure he could feel it too. He let go of my right hip and I could feel something digging into the left side of my bum. He was scratching me with his fingernail. As his nail moved from left to right, I realized he was writing.'

'He wrote on you?' said Tina, in a whisper. The skin around her neck was flushed. She was breathing heavily.

'I was going to ask him what he was writing, but it was too late. I was already cumming. As soon as I'd cum, he pulled out, ripped off the condom, and shot his spunk over my bum. I took a moment to focus on what I was feeling. My cunt was throbbing. Some of his spunk had landed on the bit he'd scratched. That stung like a bitch. But one thought was uppermost in my mind, *That's what real sex should be.*'

'I'm with you, girl,' said Tina. 'It shouldn't be about coaxing some sort of erection out of your husband and then encouraging him while he wiggles it inside you for a couple of minutes.'

'No,' Emma agreed readily. 'It should be about bracing yourself against an unstoppable force.'

'Then what happened?' asked Tina.

'He grabbed Ben's pillow and looked Ben in the eye as he wiped his prick on it. I don't know why, but that made me want him to screw me again. But he put his clothes back on and headed for the door. I still wasn't thinking straight but I managed to say, "When can I see you again?" He said, "Not sure. I'll call you sometime." And he went out. I heard the front door slam behind him. My mind was whirling, but I remembered to ask Ben what Mark had written.' She looked at him. 'What had your best friend scratched on your girlfriend's bum, Ben?'

'He'd written "SLUT," ' said Ben.

Tina said, 'Oh!' She flushed again.

'He'd scratched me so deeply that the word didn't fade for the rest of the day. I had sex with Ben yesterday evening. I made him screw me from behind so he could be reminded that I'd been with another guy—a guy who had fucked me in a way Ben could only dream about. How long did you last, Ben?'

'About a second.'

Tina went over to Emma and hugged her. The hug seemed genuine to me, free of jealousy. 'I'm proud of you, hon. You're one of us now.'

'And it feels great.'

'Any guilt?' asked Tina as she sat back down.

Emma frowned and stubbed out her cigarette. 'No, I don't think so. Maybe I've got you to thank for that. As you said, Ben wanted it as much as I did.'

'And I enjoyed it as much as you did,' said Ben, emphatically. I wasn't sure if he was trying to convince her or himself.

It was a sunny afternoon, so Tina and I decided to walk home. 'Do you want me to write "SLUT" on your ass next time we're in bed?' I asked her.

'I like the idea.' She squeezed my hand. 'But not you, babe.'

'Why not?'

'Because you wouldn't mean it. You'd write "SLUT," but you'd be thinking, *I LOVE YOU*.'

I couldn't argue with that. We walked in silence for a while.

'I've decided what I want for my birthday,' she said.

'What's that?'

'I want a Mark.'

I laughed. 'I'll have a look on Amazon. They sell everything these days.'

'I don't have any preference about color. But if they offer you a choice of size, go for XXL.'

Chapter Eight

~

'Wʜᴀᴛ ᴅɪᴅ ʏᴏᴜ ᴍᴀᴋᴇ of Adam?' Tina asked me. 'The guy from The Meeting Place? He was interesting.'

'You didn't find him creepy?'

'No, I didn't.' I thought back over our conversation with him. 'Which is odd. Because he said he'd been watching us since we came in. That should have been very psycho-stalker. Somehow it wasn't.'

'Yes, it was more like being on stage with a mentalist. I felt comfortable with him.'

'You're not thinking—?'

She waved her hand dismissively. 'Oh, no. He's not my type. I wouldn't mind spending more time with him, though. What about you?'

'It'd be interesting.'

She gave me a knowing look. 'You're on board?'

I nodded. 'Why not?'

'Good, because I've been chatting with him on the site. He's coming round for dinner tomorrow.'

'Oh, Tina. I wish you'd talk to me *before* you arrange these things.'

'Are you mad at me?'

'Yes.' But I wasn't, not really.

'Are you going to spank me?'

I laughed. 'Are you going to break my arm if I try?'

'Only one way to find out.'

I settled for kissing the top of her head.

THE NEXT EVENING, TINA and I were sitting in the den. The smell of a casserole was drifting in from the kitchen. It was five to seven. Adam was due in five minutes.

'This feels odd,' said Tina.

'What do you mean?'

'We're waiting for a man to come round; I'm wearing boring underwear and I haven't shaved my legs.'

'You'd look good dressed in a sack with hobbit feet.'

She ruffled my hair. 'That's the sort of thing only a husband says.'

The doorbell rang, and I opened the door to find Adam standing outside. He was smiling broadly and carrying two bottles of wine. 'Good evening,' he said. 'May I come in?' I stood aside and he came in. Boris approached to give him the once-over. Putting the bottles on the floor, Adam reached into his pocket and took out a paper bag. He squatted down to open the bag, which contained a fillet of cooked chicken, then pulled off strips and fed them to Boris. Between strips, he patted the dog's head. By the time Boris had finished the fillet, they were good friends. He rolled onto his back and let Adam rub his belly. 'He's a good boy,' said Adam, standing up.

'You've got past the gatekeeper,' said Tina.

'Do you always carry lumps of meat with you?' I asked.

'Only when I know I'm going to meet a dog.'

'How did you know we had a dog?'

'When we were talking in the bar, I noticed hairs on the

front of your shirt that were too coarse to be human or feline.'

He walked through the den and into the dining room, where he put his jacket over the back of the chair and the bottles on the table. 'I've brought Gewürztraminer. I think you'll like it.'

'You assume we've never tried it,' I said.

'Have you?'

'No,' I admitted.

He opened a bottle and poured us all a glass. 'To new friends,' he said. I took a sip and—damn it—it was delicious. We all sat down at the table. 'It's a nice house. You moved in here straight after you got married and never felt like leaving.'

Tina looked around the room. 'All right, what gave it away, Sherlock?'

He smiled. 'I'm flattered by the comparison. You don't have a video player in the den but you still have all your VHS box sets of *Friends* and *Buffy*. You'd have thrown those out if you'd moved.'

'We could have the video player in another room,' I pointed out.

'And do you?'

'No.'

'Can you tell what star sign I am?' asked Tina.

'No. It's ludicrous to suggest that everyone born during a certain period of the year shares recognizable traits. But I'll tell you something about your husband I've noticed.'

'What's that?'

'He doesn't have a small cock.'

'You've seen me doing the John Wayne walk to accommodate my mighty schlong?' I asked.

My sarcasm didn't rattle him a bit. 'You're not too far off. When I saw you at The Meeting Place, I did notice the way you walk, the way you carry yourself generally. It indicates a certain confidence in your body. When you went up to the bar to get the drinks, some of the women in the place were checking you out. Normally, there's a clear difference between the studs and the cucks. With you, they weren't sure. That's why you'll need to sit apart if you ever go back there. People seeing you together might well think Tina has already got her stud for the evening. They'll expect to see her real husband watching feverishly from a nearby table.'

'You're right,' said Tina. 'Rob's got a pretty big cock.' Tina was making a habit of revealing too much to people we hardly knew. But it's hard to get mad at someone who says you've got a big cock. 'His problem is he cums too quickly.'

'Tina!' I said, suddenly finding it easier to get mad at her. She'd only had a few sips of the Gewürztraminer, so she couldn't blame it on the drink this time.

'I see,' said Adam. 'Rob, can I ask what you thought when you saw Tina for the first time?'

'I thought she talked too much.'

'What did you really think?'

I took a drink and calmed down. 'I thought she was the most beautiful woman I'd ever seen.'

'Did you think you'd ever be with her?'

'No way. I assumed someone like her would already be taken.'

'Too good for you?'

'Yes.' What was it with this guy? It was as if we'd both taken truth serum.

He sat back in his chair, making himself at home. 'When you did get together, what did you think?'

'I couldn't believe my luck.'

'Is that what you were thinking the first time you had sex?'

'I kept expecting to wake up.'

'The first time was quick,' he said.

'About twelve seconds,' said Tina.

'Do you still feel like you're lucky to have her?'

'Of course I do.'

He nodded sagely. 'Well, I have a technique that could help you. Tina, you might like to go into another room for a moment. I don't think you'll like what I'm going to say.'

She picked up her glass and put her elbows on the table. 'If there's any way to stop Rob from cumming so quickly, I want to hear it,' she said.

'As you wish,' he said. 'Rob, what would you change about Tina's appearance if you could?' Before I could speak, he raised his hand. 'Don't say, "Nothing, she's perfect as she is." '

That was exactly what I was going to say. I shrugged. 'I don't know.'

'Think back to your last girlfriend before Tina. What was her name?'

'Deborah.'

'What was the most striking difference between Deborah and Tina?'

Tina snorted. 'She had *two* striking differences.'

'So her breasts were bigger than Tina's. If you're honest, do you ever miss them?'

'Well …' I began. I looked at Tina and stopped.

She took a big gulp of wine and refilled her glass. 'Go ahead, babe,' she said. 'Whatever you say, I won't hold it against you.'

'Occasionally,' I said. 'Tina's breasts are gorgeous, though.'

'I'm sure they are,' he said. 'But sometimes you wish they were bigger. So Tina's body isn't perfect. What else would you change?'

'I suppose her butt is bigger now than when I met her.'

'And you wish it was still the perfect little peach you fell in love with?'

This game was making me uncomfortable. 'Don't get me wrong. It's great the way it is now.'

'It was better in the past. You wish Tina had bigger tits and a smaller ass. Really, her body isn't that great. And you're a good-looking man with a big cock. Perhaps you could do better. Maybe *she's* the lucky one.' Tina almost choked on her drink and stared at him wide-eyed. I wasn't sure if she was annoyed or about to burst out laughing. 'Next time you're in bed, don't think, "I can't believe I'm with someone so wonderful." Think, "She is lucky to have me." '

I looked at Tina. 'Are you okay?'

She shrugged. 'Think whatever you want if it makes you fuck me until I cum. That's what I've needed ever since Steve. Anyone can lick me. I can finger myself. But at the moment, Kieran's the only one who can fuck me until I cum every time.'

'Ah, so you already have a man who fucks you until you cum every time,' Adam said, tapping his fingers on the table. 'What exactly have you needed ever since Steve?'

Tina didn't hesitate. She spoke emphatically and I noticed her fist on the table was clenched. 'I want a guy to come into our house. He doesn't say anything. He takes me by the hand and drags me up the stairs. He can't wait for me to undress so he rips off my blouse. When I'm completely naked, he gets me on my hands and knees on the bed. He doesn't bother undressing. He just unzips his trousers and gets his cock out. He fucks me hard from behind. He takes his fingernail and scratches "SLUT" or "WHORE" across my ass. He makes me cum. Then he pulls out and shoots his load all over me. He puts his cock away and leaves without saying a word.'

'Describe the blouse to me.'

'What?' She grimaced, as if he were crazy.

'You didn't say that he ripped off your top. You were very specific that it was a blouse. Describe it to me.'

'It could be anything.'

'No, it couldn't.'

'It's charcoal gray with a white diamond pattern.'

'Where did you get it?'

'Rob gave it to me for my birthday.'

'Go and put it on.'

She didn't ask why. She stood up and left the room. Adam sat there, smiling quietly and not saying anything. I looked down at the table and tried not to think about how much the blouse had cost.

When she came back down, she was wearing it. She sat.

'Why did you choose this one?' Adam asked me.

'She looks great in it.'

'Yes, she does.' He turned to Tina. 'What do you think is going to happen now?' She didn't say anything. She sat up straighter and pushed her chest towards him. Tina and I were both expecting him to rip the blouse off her. And judging by her wide eyes, parted lips, and ragged breathing, I was fairly sure that's what she wanted. Despite saying she wasn't attracted to Adam, she was turned on by what was happening. 'Tina, rip off Rob's shirt.'

She looked surprised, but she stood up and came round to my side of the table. She grabbed my shirt below the collar and pulled. The buttons flew off. Some of them landed on the table. Others clicked against the floor. She pulled the shirt off my arms and held it up in front of her. There was a seam running down the back. She used her fingernail to pick apart a couple of the stitches. This gave her a hole big enough to put two fingers in. After ripping the back of my shirt from the collar to the hem at the bottom, she threw it on the floor and stamped on it.

She was breathless and sweating a little from her exertions.

'Why did you do that?' asked Adam, although he didn't look surprised.

'You told me to.'

'I told you to rip it off. I didn't tell you to annihilate it.'

'I got carried away.' Tina did look surprised. She was even shaking slightly.

'Why do you think that is?'

She sat down and took another gulp of wine. 'Maybe I'm mad at Rob.'

'Why?' I said.

'For letting me go with other men.'

'But we—' I began.

'Yes, I know. We talked it through and agreed it was what we both wanted and yadi-yadi-ya. But can you imagine Mark letting another man fuck his wife or his girlfriend?'

'Probably not,' I agreed.

'And maybe that's one of the things hot wives like about studs? It's not only about sex. It's about feeling that here's a man who would fight for me.'

'I'd better be going,' said Adam.

'But ...' said Tina.

'You two need to be alone.'

He walked to the front door. As soon as it closed behind him, Tina said one word to me, 'Upstairs.'

Taking her hand, I dragged her up the stairs. When we got to the bedroom, she stood beside the bed. She pushed her chest towards me, and I tore the blouse off her. She pulled down her trousers, took my hand, and put it between her legs. Her panties were soaking.

'Are you still mad at me?' I asked.

'Very,' she said.

'What are you going to do about it?'

'I'm going to let you fuck me.' She used her nails to make a hole in her panties and then ripped them down the middle. 'Stick your cock in there.' Then she added with a sneer, 'Remember how lucky I am to have you.'

I threw her down on the bed, unbuckled my belt, and pulled my trousers down to my knees. My cock was hard. I lay on top of her and pushed my cock into her. But I couldn't keep it inside.

'What's the matter?' she said. 'You forgotten how to fuck?'

'Your cun ... your pussy is so wet, I keep slipping out.'

I went down and licked some of the juice out of her cunt. It was the only time I'd ever licked her to make her *less* wet. It worked. I could keep my cock inside her. I fucked her hard.

'Are you ever going to let another man fuck me again?' she asked.

'Never,' I said.

'What are you going to do to any man who looks at me?'

'Beat the shit out of him.'

'Maybe Adam was right. Maybe you *are* a stud rather than a cuck.'

This was a good thought. Unfortunately, it was too good and it started me cumming. I pulled out and ejaculated over her belly. I still hadn't made her cum using my cock. Maybe I wasn't ready to be a stud just yet. But she was so turned on that I only had to lick her for a couple of minutes until she came.

Afterwards, we lay together for a long time, not saying anything. Finally, she asked, 'Did you enjoy that, babe?'

'Err … I think so.'

'You do realize I said those things in the heat of passion? I'm still going to fuck other men.'

'Of course. And on that subject, Adam …' I began.

'What about him?'

'When you thought he was about to rip off your blouse, you were looking at him the way Boris looks at a chicken fillet. I got the feeling that if he'd put the moves on you, you'd have responded.'

She frowned reflectively for a moment. 'Probably.'

'I thought you weren't interested in him that way.'

'When he was just a guy in a bar, I wasn't. But … I've spent less than an hour with him in total. Already it feels like he knows me better than anyone—except you, of course.'

'Of course. But if he's Mister Insight, he must have known he could fuck you if he wanted to. He just left.'

'You think he's not really into me? He's playing games with us?'

'Maybe he likes being the fly on the wall. He observes, but he doesn't get involved himself.'

'He didn't even stay for dinner.' Her eyes suddenly widened. 'Dinner! The casserole's still in the oven.'

She leapt out of bed and grabbed her robe from the hook behind the door. She was still slipping it on as she ran down the stairs. I hoped we hadn't left any drapes open. Putting on my robe, I followed with less urgency. I picked my shirt buttons off the dining room floor so the dog wouldn't eat them. Tina put the casserole on the table. It was burnt around the edges, but still good. The second bottle of Gewürztraminer was on the table, so we drank it as we ate. We played a game we'd invented called In The Event of a Fire. Taking turns, we asked each other, 'In the event of a fire, which five books would you save? Which five albums would you save?' and so on. After an hour, we were down to asking things like, 'Which five breakfast cereals would you save?'

Boris lay on the floor between us, sleeping contentedly. He knew he'd be the first thing both of us would save in the event of a fire.

Chapter Nine

~

'I'VE GOT AN IDEA about how we can spice things up with Kieran,' said Tina.

I gave her a quizzical look. 'Who do you want at the moment—Kieran, Mark, or Adam?'

She folded her arms across her chest, a bit defensively. 'Why do I have to choose? I thought it was the hot wife's prerogative to fuck whoever she damn well pleased.'

'I don't think anyone's written a rule book.'

'I'm fascinated by Adam. I've got a feeling that sex with him would go to dark places. Mark has a great body and—if we believe Emma—he's also a pretty intense fuck. And Kieran has—'

I held up a hand to stop her. 'Yes, we all know what Kieran has. What's your plan for spicing things up?'

'Where did we put that camcorder we had with us in Paris?'

This worried me immediately. 'Not sure. We definitely had it in the luggage when we came home. But we never watched any of the stuff we filmed there.'

'Can you have a look for it? I think you should start filming Kieran and me together.'

'No, no, no.' I couldn't stop shaking my head.

'Why not? It would be exciting.'

'Tina, don't you remember what it was like when you let Steve take photos of you? He blackmailed you and you nearly lost your job.'

'We made the mistake of letting him keep the photos. We'll hang onto the films ourselves.'

'What if Kieran wants a copy?'

' "Not my scene," ' she said, in her best Kieran voice. 'Think about it, babe. After Kieran goes, you love it when I tell you all about it. You always want to hear how good it felt. Now imagine watching me with him. I can't think of anything better than riding you or jerking you off while we watch Kieran fucking me. I want to see what you see. I want to watch myself being fucked.' She felt my cock through my trousers. 'You can't pretend you don't like the idea.'

I was getting annoyed with my cock. He kept going against my better judgement. 'I have a feeling it's another of those ideas which is better as a fantasy than as reality.'

'I don't see what can go wrong.'

'Why do those sound like famous last words?'

On Wednesday, we were preparing for Kieran to come round. Tina wanted to look good for the camera, so she put on a lot more makeup than normal. She wore a white blouse that was tied into a knot under her breasts to show off her well-toned midriff.

'I really should have my bellybutton pierced for the complete porno look,' she said. She put on a short navy skirt over the white stockings—she knew they weren't negotiable.

When he arrived, she was standing in the hall. 'How do I look?' she said.

'Great,' he said. 'Any special reason?'

'Do you want to be a star?'

'What do you mean?'

'Well, Rob was rummaging in the attic the other day and he found our old movie camera. Would it be okay if he filmed us?'

'Do I have to do anything different?' he asked. He really did not like the idea of change.

'No, do what you normally do. Rob isn't going to shout "Cut!" at a crucial moment.'

He shrugged. 'I don't mind.'

The three of us went upstairs. I stood in the corner of the bedroom with the camera. I should have practiced before Kieran arrived. The trip to Paris had been eight months ago and I hadn't used the camera since. I was finding it hard to zoom in smoothly on anything. Kieran started undressing. He was playing along enough to face the camera as he took off his clothes. I managed an in-focus shot of him pulling down his shorts and got a full frame close-up of his erect cock. He stood still for a moment so I could linger on that shot. We both knew Tina would enjoy it. Then I panned the camera round to Tina, who'd decided to act like she didn't know the camera was there. She removed her clothes unselfconsciously, like she was just getting ready for bed. Even though I knew she was playacting, I enjoyed filming her undressing like no one was watching.

She lay down. It was more difficult for her to pretend that nothing was happening when a naked Kieran joined her on the bed. He did what he always did. He licked her cunt, making sure she was wet enough for him. He knew where his condoms were by now, so he reached for one and put it on. He penetrated her slowly, giving her time to accommodate his size. They had developed a simple code. Once he was all the way in, he looked her in the eye. She nodded to tell him she was all right and he wasn't hurting her. He kissed her neck and started thrusting into her, maintaining a steady rhythm with no variation until she came. I was jealous of him. It wasn't only his huge cock, but also the way he fucked her with no problems and no doubts, knowing he could get it up every time, knowing he wouldn't cum until she was satisfied. He could be counted on to do a good job.

After Kieran had gone, I hooked up the camera to the television in the den so we could watch our movie.

Tina had worn her robe downstairs. As the film started, she let it fall to the floor. I took my clothes off. We sat on the couch and looked at the screen. The start of the film was a surreal montage of blurred images. The first proper shot was of Kieran undressing. Our camera was never of the highest quality and several months of sitting unloved in a closet hadn't done it any good. The picture was rather fuzzy, but we could still see Kieran's cock emerging from his shorts. 'It is magnificent, isn't it, babe?' she said.

'It's a lot bigger than mine.'

Tina took hold of my cock and worked the head between her finger and thumb. 'It's not just bigger, it's better. It looks better. It tastes better. It feels better when I'm letting him fuck me. I'm so much in love with his cock.'

'Are you in love with mine?'

'No,' she said. She paused and looked at me, as if wondering how far she could go. 'I hate it.'

'Did you think that the first time you saw it?'

She nodded. 'You took your clothes off and posed like you had something to be proud of. All I could think was, "What the fuck am I supposed to do with that?" ' She put her hand around my cock and started jerking it hard. 'It's not big enough for me and you don't know how to use it.' I was breathing heavily. She stopped and grinned. 'Time out, babe. You're getting over-excited. I don't want this to end yet.'

We sat back and watched the film for a while. Kieran was licking Tina's cunt. 'You are better at licking me than he is,' she said, throwing me a bone.

'It's not a skill you need to develop when you've got a cock like his.'

'Have you calmed down a bit?'

I was sitting next to my naked wife while watching a man perform cunnilingus on her. I wasn't exactly calm. But I said, 'Yes, I'm fine.'

'Good, because I want you to fuck me.'

She stood with her back to me. I moved my butt closer to the front of the couch. That straightened out my body and pointed my cock at the ceiling. I couldn't resist reaching forward to cup those gorgeous buttocks. As I felt her womanly ass, I regretted ever implying that it was better when it was smaller. She walked backwards with my legs between hers and lowered herself down slowly. I held the base of my cock so I could guide the tip into her cunt. When I was fully inside her, she sat with her back against my chest. I reached my hand around and played with her clit. On the screen, Kieran had started to fuck her.

'I can really feel your cock, babe,' said Tina. That sounded like a compliment. 'Probably because I'm still deliciously sore from the pounding Kieran gave me.' Okay, it was a backhanded compliment, but I took what I could get.

We looked at the screen again to see Tina with her eyes closed and her mouth slightly open. I hadn't noticed it before, but Kieran did speed up his thrusts a little as he sensed she was about to cum. I increased the speed of my hand on her clit to match what was happening on the screen. She was breathing heavily. I rubbed her clit as fast as I could, using my other hand to tug on her left nipple. The on-screen Tina cried out her orgasm. At the same time, the live Tina sitting on my cock arched her back and shouted, 'Yes!' Her cunt pulsed around my cock as she came.

She threw her head back onto my shoulder. 'Thank you, babe,' she said, kissing my cheek.

'Does that count as making you cum with my cock?'

'Mm, you were also fingering my clit. Plus we were watching pretty hot porn.'

'But technically you did cum with my cock inside you.'

'Okay, babe, we'll count that as a win. Hey, the film's not finished yet.'

Kieran had pulled out of Tina and was kneeling on the bed beside her, level with her chest. She pushed her tits together and he was pointing his cock at them. He jerked his cock vigorously for a couple of minutes and came with his usual flood. Only now did Tina start playing up for the camera. She sat up and put her hands under her boobs, offering her semen-coated tits to the camera. Moving her hands away, she let the cum run down her breasts and onto her belly. When some of it fell on her thighs, she scooped up a drip with her finger. She gave the camera her most wicked look and licked his cum off her finger, running her tongue round her lips like it was the most delicious thing she'd ever tasted.

She lay down on the floor in front of the couch, and I knelt beside her. She pushed her tits together, like she was doing on screen. I could see she still had some of Kieran's dried cum on them. 'Come on, babe,' said Tina. 'Mix yours with his. I'll have two men's seed on my tits. How slutty will I be then?'

Hearing this was too much for me. I came over my wife. My cock wasn't as big as the one on the screen; the live Tina had less than half the cum on her that she had on the screen. But it's always difficult to recreate what you see in a porn movie.

'So, babe, was the camcorder a good idea?' she asked, sitting up.

'Yes,' I was forced to admit.

'Because I've got to tell you, I enjoyed watching the movie with you even more than I enjoyed making it. And I've got to insult your cock more often. That was hot.'

'Yes, it was.'

'Am I a kinky bitch?'

'We both are.'

'And we wouldn't have it any other way. Let's build up a library of my exploits and watch them when I'm too old to do anything more. Shall we watch the film of Paris now?'

After we cleaned up and got dressed, she let Boris back into the den and gave him a chew treat for being so patient. We thought it would be a good idea to have an evening without wine, so I made two cups of tea.

We spent the rest of the evening in the den with our dog and watched ourselves in Paris. I'd spent most of the time behind the camera, so there were a lot of shots of Tina. Tina posing under the Arc de Triomphe. Tina on top of Montmartre with the city laid out beneath her. Tina coming out of Galeries Lafayette, having spent far too much on underwear. Anyone who saw us in Paris would have thought we were an ordinary, loving couple. As we walked along the Champs Elysées holding hands, no one would have suspected that I loved watching her getting fucked by big-cocked men. And anyone who saw us now, watching home movies and drinking tea, would never guess that half an hour ago, she'd been telling me how much she hated my cock.

After the film was over, we went upstairs for an early night. Tina sat on the bed. She had a bottle of baby oil on her bedside table. She put a few drops on a cotton wool ball and dragged it across her eyes. Ten minutes later, she'd removed all her makeup. She was my naturally beautiful wife again. We got into bed. I put my arm around her and we went to sleep.

Chapter Ten

~

GODDESSE HAS ENTERED THE *chat room.*

GoddessE: *Hey, Tina. How's it going?*

hotwife37: *Great. How are you?*

GoddessE: *Wonderful. I've got some fantastic news to share with you.*

hotwife37: *???*

GoddessE: *I'd prefer to tell you in person. We owe you a dinner. Are you and Rob around next Friday?*

hotwife37: *7:30 ok?*

GoddessE: *perfect*

hotwife37: *You want us to come over to your place?*

GoddessE: *No. We want to take you out. Do you know L'Oie Qui Fume?*

'Ever heard of it?' she asked me.

'Yes. I see it on my way to work every day. It's one of those places where the salad costs the same as a small car.'

'She said they owe us a dinner. That means they're paying, right?'

'Pretty sure it does. If not, we can offer to do the dishes.'

'Or I can fuck the manager.'

'There's always a solution if you look hard enough. And at least if we're at a classy restaurant, Ben will have to keep it in his pants.'

hotwife37: *Yes, it's our favorite. We go there all the time.*

GoddessE: *The quail's eggs are to die for, aren't they?*

hotwife37: *I couldn't live without them.*

GoddessE: *Great! See you on Friday.*

GoddessE has left the room.

'We're moving up in the world, babe,' said Tina. 'Dig out your suit and give it the best ironing it's ever had. We have to look like we belong there.'

THE HEAD WAITER KNEW immediately that I did not belong there. We'd spent a lot of money over the past year making Tina look good, but we'd never thought much about my appearance. She looked fabulous in the scarlet dress she'd worn to her company ball the year before. But my black suit was shiny after too many visits to the dry cleaner's. The waiter was debating whether to let us in or not. Then Emma waved to us and shouted across the room, 'Tina! Rob! Over here!' We went over to their table. I kissed Emma on both cheeks and shook Ben's hand. I could see the waiter thinking he'd have to put up with me if they were my friends.

We sat down. It was a wonderful place with low, relaxing lighting. The carpet was a deep red. One wall was glass with a small fig tree growing behind it. Emma pointed to a bowl in the middle of our table. It was full of quail's eggs for us to pick at like they were olives. Ben reached for the half-empty bottle of champagne chilling in a bucket next to the table and poured us each a glass.

'Well, don't keep us in suspense,' said Tina. 'What's the big news?'

Emma held out her left hand. She was wearing a ring with an enormous diamond on it. I thought it looked duller than most new rings look, but I didn't say anything. Tina let out a scream. She stood up and ran round the table to kiss both of them. 'Ben popped the question two days ago,' said Emma. 'I didn't hesitate for a second.'

'That's wonderful,' said Tina. We all drank a toast to the happy couple. 'Have you set a date yet?'

'Probably about a month from now,' said Emma.

'That's quick,' said Tina. 'You're not …?'

Emma laughed. 'Oh, no! Nothing like that. Ben's dad has said he's going to sort everything out. Apparently, he's good at getting things done quickly.'

'When my sister got married, he got the whole thing arranged in a couple of weeks,' said Ben.

'Do you know where it's going to be?'

'My dad's got a couple of places he likes.'

'You should get to choose,' said Tina to Emma. 'It's your day.'

Emma made a face. 'But it's John's money.' She paused and looked down at the table. 'It is generous of him to pay for everything. My dad thought it would be up to him. He lost everything in the 2008 crash. I dread to think where we'd have the wedding if *my* family were paying for it.'

Ben put his hand on her shoulder. 'My dad's happy to do it,' he said. 'He loves organizing things. The place where Paige—that's my sister—got married was great. It didn't stop her complaining, of course. But, if it's anything like that, I'll be happy.'

'Err … have you told Mark?' asked Tina.

'Oh yes,' said Ben. 'He's agreed to be my best man.'

'I was worried about how he'd react when I told him,' said Emma. 'But he took it well. He came round last night. The three of us sat down in the living room. I said, "Well, congratulate us," and showed him the ring. He didn't say anything. He motioned me to sit next to him on the couch. At first, I thought he was angry. Then he said, "You're in love with Ben?" I looked him in the eye and said, "Yes, I love him so much." He pulled my head towards his and kissed me. I opened my mouth wide and he pushed his tongue in against mine. He'd been drinking beer. Usually I hate beer but I love tasting it in Mark's mouth. He undid the buttons of my cardigan and put his hand inside my bra. "You're totally committed to him," he said, as he felt up my breasts. He put his hand up my skirt and got hold of my knickers. I raised my bum off the couch, so he could pull them down. He lifted my skirt up to my waist and unzipped his jeans. "I'm a respectable engaged woman," I said, spreading my legs for him. "Soon to become a respectable married woman," he replied, as he unzipped his trousers and stuck his prick into me.'

I was starting to get nervous. If Emma was happy to talk like this in the restaurant, I couldn't rule out the possibility that she'd make Ben get his cock out.

Emma carried on. 'He screwed me hard and he,' she blushed, 'he called me a whore.' *That* was the bit that made her blush? 'Then he pulled out, sat beside me again, and told me to wank him off. I asked him where he wanted to cum, even though I already knew. I stroked his prick with my right hand. When his eyes narrowed and he was about to shoot, I rested the tip of his prick on the diamond of my engagement ring. He came all over it. His spunk covered the stone and trickled down over the band. I held it up to show it to both of them. Mark said, "I look forward to doing the same to your wedding ring. If you think a little thing like you getting married is going to stop what we've got going on, you must be stupid." I reassured him, "I love being a hot girlfriend and I'm going to enjoy being a hot wife even more." Then I put my knickers back on and did up my cardigan. Mark put his prick away, and we all started acting like normal people. Mark shook Ben's hand and said, "Congratulations! She's a lovely girl. Take good care of her." Then he kissed me on the cheek and said, "Ben's my best friend. Make him happy." We all sat down, had a drink, and Mark talked about the anecdotes he could use in his best man's speech.'

'It's a pity all his anecdotes seem to involve him humiliating me in some way,' said Ben. He was obviously apprehensive about what Mark would say. But then he gave me a pointed look. He knew I understood that he was also turned on by the thought.

'I'm sure they'll get big laughs at the wedding breakfast,' said Emma.

'Not from my dad.'

'I've decided I'm going to make a speech too,' said Emma. 'The men get to talk while the women sit quiet and look pretty? Not at my wedding.'

'You go, girl,' said Tina. 'Who are your bridesmaids?'

'My cousin, Rebecca, and my best friend, Abi. And I've got a favor to ask you, Tina. I know we haven't been friends all that long. But you already know more about me than most people. And you understand our lifestyle better than anyone. Tina, would you be my matron of honor?'

Tina didn't say anything. She ran round to the other side of the table again and gave Emma another kiss. We all took that as a yes.

'You will have rather specific duties,' said Emma, when Tina had sat down again. 'Ben and I have talked a lot about this. I'm going to spend the night before the wedding with Mark. I might be tired for my wedding day, but I'm sure adrenaline will pull me through. Then Mark and I need to have some time on the wedding morning. Ben has made a special request.' She looked at Ben. 'Do you want to tell them?'

It was Ben's turn to blush. He leaned forward and lowered his voice. 'As you can imagine, we've spent a lot of time fantasizing about our wedding. There's one idea that drives me crazy. I want Emma to have Mark's cum on her tits when we get married. I want to know that she has the proof of her infidelity right there on her body as she says her vows to me.'

Tina's eyes widened and she bit her lip. 'That's so hot.'

'Who am I to deny my husband?' said Emma. 'I'm also going

to ask Mark to give me a couple of love bites in intimate places. I'm not saying where. We need to keep a few surprises for our wedding night.'

'So you two *will* be together that night?' asked Tina.

'I know it's a bit conventional,' said Emma, 'but there is a tiny conservative part of me that says I should be with my husband on our wedding night and during our honeymoon. But back to the morning. I love Rebecca and Abi to bits, but they will never understand this lifestyle. They're the sort of girls who'll think it's fun to burst into the bride's room at eight in the morning with a bottle of champagne. I need you to keep them occupied. You can set them to design a floral headdress for me. Tell them it's important to me that it's personally made by my friends. Get them to make it and remake it until I give you the all-clear.'

'Good idea,' said Tina.

'Keep your phone on you. I'll call you as soon as Mark's out of the way and I've covered up the evidence. Then you can unleash the girls and they can do what they want.'

'Got it.'

'It is crucial that no one finds out about Emma and Mark,' said Ben. He paused, his expression downcast. Emma reached for his hand and squeezed it. 'My parents divorced when I was twelve.'

Tina and I both murmured, 'Sorry to hear that.'

'In reality, there were loads of reasons why. My dad can't see that. For him, it all came down to one thing. My mom had an affair. Ever since then, he spits blood at any mention of infidelity. He most definitely would not accept any of this.'

'So we've got to keep everything under wraps,' said Emma. 'You're the only people we can trust to do that.'

The waiter arrived to take our order. I asked for the cheapest thing on the menu, in case we ended up paying. Tina had no such worries. She ordered the steak with three different side dishes. When the champagne bottle was empty, Emma picked it up and waved it at the waiter. He replaced it with a full one.

As we ate, Ben told us about his job, working for his father. I got the impression he hadn't had any choice about it. As the only son, he was being groomed to take over the business one day. Emma asked about my teaching. Tina talked about her boss, David, and their relationship, which had grown into love-hate after years of pure hate. I found myself liking Ben and Emma more and more. They were nice people. We were from different worlds, but I could imagine us being friends even if we didn't have one special thing in common.

After we'd finished dessert, Emma said, 'We always like to finish with a brandy. It keeps us warm on the way home.'

'Sounds great,' said Tina.

Emma signaled to the head waiter. 'Four brandies, please.'

He looked at me with a smirk. 'Which brand do you prefer, sir?'

I was grateful to my French colleague, Danielle. She'd told me about her father, who was a keen brandy drinker. One name stuck in my mind. 'Do you have any François Voyer?' I asked the waiter, nonchalantly. I was delighted to see his eyebrows go up.

'Oh, that's lovely,' said Emma. 'Yes, four of those.'

We drank the brandies slowly. I had inadvertently made an excellent choice. 'Anyone want anything else?' asked Ben.

Tina and I patted our bellies in unison. 'I'm stuffed,' I said.

'Couldn't eat another thing,' said Tina.

Ben asked the waiter for the bill. I made a feint of reaching for my wallet. 'Let me help you out,' I said.

Ben waved me away. 'This one's on us.'

'We'll get the next one,' said Tina.

'Although it'll probably be at Pizza Hut,' I muttered. Tina heard me and grinned. My voice didn't make it across the table.

Ben casually dropped his credit card onto the bill. Outside the restaurant, we thanked them profusely. 'It was nothing,' said Emma. Well, it was nothing for *her*. Ben had paid.

*

An hour later, Tina and I were in bed. 'You seemed to like the idea of Emma getting married with another man's cum on her tits,' I said.

Tina bit her lip again. 'I loved it. Do you wish we'd done that at our wedding?'

'That would have been good. But I'd rather have tasted another man when I kissed the bride.'

'You wanted me to stop off on the way to my wedding and suck another guy's cock? That would have made me the sluttiest bride ever.'

I kissed her and tried to imagine how that would taste. 'Can we get divorced and remarried on the same day so you can do that?'

'You'll have to settle for me being the sluttiest matron of honor ever. I've got an important job to do the evening of the wedding.'

'You mean the morning.'

'I mean the evening. You heard what Emma said. She wants to be with Ben on their wedding night. Why do you think she told me that? She wants me to look after Mark.'

Tina was planning to steal Emma's stud on her wedding day? I didn't see how that could possibly end well. But my cock, still refusing to be sensible, was instantly fully erect. 'I don't think that's what she meant at all.'

'You've got to pick up on the subtext, babe. There's a fine old tradition of the best man sleeping with the matron of honor.'

'I thought it was the bridesmaid.'

'Close enough. I will be proud to uphold that tradition. And you're going to get it all on film. That's one I'll want to watch over and over again. Are you hard?'

'Yes,' I said.

'Good,' she said. 'Lie on your back.'

I did what she asked. Lowering her cunt onto my cock, she closed her eyes and rode up and down on me, rubbing her clit.

I wasn't fucking her. She was using my cock to masturbate with while she imagined herself with Mark.

And at that moment, I didn't mind at all.

Chapter Eleven

~

KIERAN HAD LEFT TWENTY minutes ago. Tina and I had finished having sex. This was normally a time when we talked, but she was staring at the ceiling in silence. 'How you doing?' I asked at last.

'Fine,' she said, uncertainly. 'Stay there, babe.' She got up, put on her bathrobe, and went downstairs. She left the door open, so Boris wandered in and lay down beside the bed. When she came back, she was carrying a bottle of wine and two glasses. She poured me a large one.

'There's no point getting me drunk,' I told her. 'You've already had your way with me.'

She smiled thinly and poured one for herself. She sat down on the bed and bent down to tickle Boris behind the ear. 'I think it's time to cut down on Kieran's visits.'

'Up to you,' I said. 'It seems harsh to break up with him half an hour after he made you cum.'

'I'm not going to break up with him. He still has a fantastic instrument, even if he can only play one tune on it. Maybe I'll see him once a month. I want to look forward to it. At the moment, it's, "Oh, it's Wednesday, Kieran's coming round." It's just another part of my week—like laundry night.'

'Who are you going to focus on? Mark? Adam?' I tried a long shot. 'Me?'

She was silent for a second. She drank half the wine in her glass. 'Guess who I saw at work today.'

It was obvious from her tone of voice. 'Steve.'

'I suppose it was inevitable I'd run into him, but it was still a shock. Ever since David reassigned him, I've managed to avoid him. Today, I stepped into the elevator and there he was.'

'Did you punch him in the face?'

'No. There were a couple of other people in the elevator. As a manager, I'm supposed to set an example. He looked at me and nodded like we were old acquaintances.' She paused and topped up her glass. 'I hate that guy so much.'

'So do I.'

'But … do you remember when he used to come round? When we were waiting for him, I got so horny, I couldn't sit still. Then he arrived and I never knew what he was going to do. It was that roller coaster feeling. A little bit scary but so exciting. I don't get that with Kieran. I'll never forgive Steve for what he did to us. But there is part of me—'

I held up my hand. 'Oh, Tina, no.'

'It didn't end well with him.'

I stared at her, wide-eyed. 'What, when he blackmailed us and you almost lost your job? No, not the best way to finish a relationship.'

'I think maybe I need closure.'

'Let's hire a hitman. You can't get better closure than that.'

'I know he's a bastard. I also know he's the best sex I've ever had. Just once more, I need to feel—'

'No, Tina.'

Her eyes hardened. 'Rob, I love you but I've made up my mind. I need to get him out of my system. I can either do it here and you can watch, or I can go to his place.'

I could see her mind was made up, but I felt I should try.

'Tina, it's not a good idea to get involved with him again.'

'I'm not getting "involved with him again." It's only going to happen once.'

That was like hearing an alcoholic say he was only going to have one drink.

WHEN SHE CAME HOME the next day, Tina was tight-lipped. She said, 'I did it. I sent Steve an email. It read, *Hi Steve, It was good to see you in the elevator the other day. Still spending a lot of time at the gym, I see. I'm sorry that things went so badly wrong between us. Would you like to come round to our place on Friday evening? Let's have one last good experience.*'

'I can't believe you apologized to him,' I said.

'Nor can I. You do what you have to do. But it was clear, wasn't it? I mean, he must have known what I was talking about?'

'Sure.'

'He sent me a reply less than a minute later.'

She went silent, so I pressed her. 'And? What did he say?'

She looked at me with angry tears in her eyes. 'He said no.'

Chapter Twelve

~

ON THE DAY BEFORE the wedding, Tina and I took the afternoon off work. Boris saw us packing a suitcase and knew what was happening. He rubbed his head against our legs and made his eyes as big as possible. As we set off, he sat moping in the back of the car, though he perked up when we arrived at Louise's house. She was pleased to see him, too. She'd been lonely since she and her husband had split up. I crouched down in her hallway and patted Boris's head. 'You be a good boy, buddy. I'll see you on Sunday.' Louise distracted him with a tennis ball, while I made good my escape.

The rehearsal was due to start at six. We didn't want to be late so we'd allowed four hours for a drive that took us less than two and arrived at the hotel just after half past three. As I steered the car up the curved driveway, I realized this was not the sort of hotel we normally frequented. I parked our car under a tree at the back and hoped nobody would notice it. Once we'd passed through the revolving door into the lobby, I noticed a sculpture of nine young women who might have been Muses, lit by a huge chandelier. The walls were crimson, and the carpet was a gold and red Asian textile pattern. Opposite the main entrance were two wide spiral staircases.

'I think we took a wrong turning,' I muttered to Tina. 'We've ended up at Elton John's house.'

A man in a suit that matched the walls was standing behind the reception desk. I started towards him but I was stopped by a tall man who came striding into the lobby. He was talking rapidly into his phone. When he saw us, he held up a finger, telling us to wait a moment. He finished his call and smiled warmly at us. His gray hair was so carefully sculpted that it looked plastic. He was wearing a blue pinstripe suit with a white shirt and a blue silk tie. His suit didn't just fit: it fitted perfectly, as if it had been made to measure that morning. He had the easy confidence of someone who knows he's the richest man in the place, and a smile that made me want to buy something from him.

'I'm John, Ben's father,' he said, and kissed Tina on the lips. She was surprised but didn't seem to mind. 'You're the first guests to arrive. You must be Tina. We're going to have to dress you in a sack or you'll overshadow Emma. You are beautiful.'

Tina blushed. 'Thank you.'

He shook my hand. 'What do you do?'

'I'm a teacher.'

'Good for you. Doing a job that makes a difference and to hell with the money. Never something I could do myself. Now let me show you the set-up we've got here.' He led us through glass doors into a vast dining room. There was activity everywhere. People in crimson suits were cleaning, polishing, and decorating. A huge picture of Emma and Ben hung on the wall facing the door. 'We're going to eat in here tomorrow. The chef I've got has two Michelin stars. Though I never understood why a tire company knows anything about food.'

There were three doors at the back of the room. He took us through one of them into a smaller room with chairs neatly laid out on either side of a strip of white carpet. The carpet led to an archway made out of white roses. A large mahogany table doubled as an altar, and there was an organ against the side wall. More people in crimson suits were shampooing the carpet and spritzing the roses with water. 'The service will be in here. Four o'clock sharp. A firing squad is on standby for anyone who gets dirt on the carpet.' We followed him into another huge room that had a dance floor and a stage. 'We're having "You To Me Are Everything" for the first dance. Emma wanted something by a group called Lonestar, but who's ever heard of them?' He led us back into the dining room and through the other door, where tables were laid out for roulette, blackjack, and craps. 'After dinner, you're free to try your luck in here. Well, I say "free." You play with real money and who knows? You might win some real money. Now, let me take you upstairs.'

We went back into the lobby and John called over to the man at reception, 'Four-two-six!' The man stood to attention at the sound of John's voice. He grabbed a couple of key cards and sprinted over to where we were standing. John took the cards and pressed the button to call the elevator.

'As matron of honor, you get a premier suite,' he said. 'You can stay in it, too,' he added to me.

'Thanks,' I said, trying to keep my voice irony-free.

We went up to the fourth floor. 'You should be comfortable here.' He opened the door and showed us into the suite. We went into the living room, where two three-seater couches in beige leather were arranged around a marble-topped coffee table. In the next room was a table with six chairs, in case we wanted to host a dinner party while we were staying there. We followed John into the bedroom. He flicked a switch and a big chandelier lit up the room. Fifty people could have slept on the floor without spooning. The king-sized double bed was covered in crisp white sheets and a quilt in a deep brown. In front of the bed was a chaise longue, and next to the window, a desk with a padded wooden chair under it. A huge walk-in closet dominated the wall opposite the bed. John opened the closet door. Tina's dress was the only thing hanging in it. It was a strapless, sleeveless floor-length dress in purple silk with a large bow on the left hip.

'Beautiful!' said Tina.

'If you look too good in it, I'll put a pair of Mickey Rooney glasses on you and black out a couple of your teeth,' he said.

'Don't worry,' said Tina. 'It's Emma's day.'

'It's Ben's day too. How do you like the room?'

'It's amazing,' said Tina.

He turned to me. 'You may want to take some photos to show the other teachers at your school. They might not have seen a place like this before. Well, I'll leave you to get settled in. I want all members of the wedding party in place by a quarter to six at the latest. It's a full dress rehearsal with everyone wearing exactly what they'll wear tomorrow—except Emma, of course. I'm not having Ben see her dress before the day itself.'

He went out.

'He was a star turn,' said Tina.

'Patronizing bastard,' was my response.

'Rob! He's paying for us to stay in this place.'

'I wonder what he wants in return. He obviously likes you.'

'Do you think so?' she said, with a smile.

'He's worried you're going to steal Emma's thunder. You're going to be the most beautiful woman at the wedding.'

'Do you think Mark will want me?'

'Of course he will.'

'But Steve—'

'We've established many times that Steve is an idiot.'

She looked around the room. 'This is perfect for us, babe. You have your choice of two sofas and a chaise longue if you find the bed occupied. And ...' She picked up the chair from behind the desk and carried it over to the closet. There was more than enough room for the chair inside. 'You can sit in there. You'll have a perfect view. You can film everything. Mark will never know.'

'What happens afterwards? I don't want to spend the night in there.'

'Why not? The closet's bigger than our bedroom at home. Don't worry. He'll leave straight afterwards or he'll go to sleep. Either way, you'll be able to get out. Now, I want you to help me get ready. There's probably a bath the size of an Olympic swimming pool around here somewhere.'

We went into the bathroom, which was largely done in black and white marble with an oval bath in the middle. On a small table next to the bath was a vase filled with fresh roses and a number of bottles. Tina unscrewed a bottle of bath gel and sniffed it. 'Oh, smell that, babe. Lemon and coconut. I could drink that straight from the bottle.'

She ran the bath and poured half the bottle into it. Taking her clothes off, she climbed in and lay there with only her head above the water. 'What shaving stuff have they got in here?' she asked.

There was a leather box in a cabinet by the basin. Inside was a straight razor, a brush, and a tub of shaving cream. I showed Tina the razor. 'I've never used one of these before. They're supposed to give you a really close shave.'

She raised her arms above her head. 'Do my pits, babe.'

By most standards, her pits were already well shaved, but she wanted them to be perfect. I knelt beside the bath and smeared cream under her arms, where there was just a tiny bit of stubble. I felt nervous, applying a razor blade to my wife's body. By the time I'd finished, her pits were totally smooth and there wasn't so much as a nick in her skin.

'You're good at this,' she said. She paused for a moment. 'You know, from what Emma was saying, Mark isn't a big fan of hair.'

'You want me to shave your legs, as well?'

'No, they're fine. I'm thinking … of somewhere else.'

'Really? You've never done that before.'

'I feel like I need a USP—to make Mark want me more.'

'If he gets as far as knowing that you've shaved pubes, you can be fairly sure he wants you.'

She used her big toe to pull the lever that released the plug. The water level dropped. When her pubes were above water, she put the plug back in. 'Are you sure you want me taking a straight razor to you down there?' I asked.

'I wouldn't trust anyone else to do it.'

Her pubes were already soft from the hot water and the bath gel, but I still used a lot of shaving cream. I gently dragged the razor across them. A clump of hair floated away. I worked slowly, feeling like a sculptor, carefully removing every piece to reveal the perfection beneath. I rubbed my finger over the whole area. A few strands remained here and there so I took them off with deft strokes of the blade. Finally, everything was completely smooth.

There were islands of her pubes floating on the water. 'We could sell those on eBay,' she suggested.

'Is that how you want to make your fortune?'

'Okay, pull the plug.' After the water had run away, she stood up. 'How do I look, babe?'

I felt the way she'd felt about men with hairy chests. I'd never thought about shaving as something that would turn me on. But she looked wonderfully sexy with a hairless cunt. 'You look great,' I said.

'Is it making you horny?'

'Oh yes.'

'Take your pants off and lie on the floor.'

I took *all* my clothes off and lay on my back with my cock standing up, hard and straight. She stepped out of the bath and quickly dried herself. She stood over me with her feet on either side of my hips. Tina had thigh muscles to rival Beyoncé's and she was able to lower her cunt towards my cock slowly. She knew how much I loved this and she'd done it hundreds of times. I was used to feeling her pubes tickling the tip of my cock. This time, the first thing I felt was the exquisite softness of her cunt lips.

'How badly do you want to fuck my completely naked pussy?'

'I *need* to fuck it,' I said.

She stood up in one swift movement. 'Sorry, you can't. We've got to go to the rehearsal.'

THERE WERE LOTS OF people in the room that was doubling as the chapel. Tina wasn't sure where she was supposed to be, so we hung back by the door as she scanned the room. I knew who she was looking for. 'There he is,' she said quietly, 'talking to Ben. He's even more gorgeous in real life. There's something about a bad boy in a suit.'

Mark did look good. His large, powerful body was covered by an expensive, well-made suit, and his dark brown hair was cut very short. He looked like a sportsman at an awards ceremony. He had the assured, self-satisfied demeanor of a best man who's fucking the bride.

Tina whispered in my ear, 'That man is going to have the best night of his life tomorrow. His cock is going in my mouth, between my tits, up my pussy, and up my ass.'

'Tina!' I whispered back. 'I'm wearing suit trousers. You can't hide a bulge in these.'

She grinned. 'Sorry, babe, let's focus on the rehearsal.'

A woman walked in. She had long, dark hair, a sharp nose, and lips that looked permanently pursed. Her brows were high and looping, just like Ben's. While they made him appear surprised, she seemed disgusted with everything. Tina smiled at her. 'You must be Ben's sister. Paige, right?'

Paige didn't answer straightaway. She looked Tina up and down. 'And you must be the one Emma prefers to me.'

'I'm sorry?'

'Emma promised me that if she and Ben ever got married, *I'd* be her matron of honor. God help my brother if that's how much her promises are worth.'

There were good reasons why Emma had changed her mind. Tina couldn't really share them with Paige.

'I didn't even have a matron of honor,' continued Paige. 'Daddy said I could only have two bridesmaids. But nothing's too good for Ben's golden girl. Look at this place. When I got married, the canopy was made of ribbons. Fucking ribbons. I might have liked some roses, but no one asked me.'

John's voice rang out across the room. 'All members of the wedding party to me, please.'

'Daddy's calling you,' said Paige. 'Run along. It's not like *I'm* in the wedding party.'

Tina joined the group around John. Paige sat down next to a man with a beard and a ponytail. I guessed he was the husband who'd also suffered the humiliation of marrying under ribbons. I wanted to sit as far from them as possible so I sat next to a woman with short, curly black hair. 'Are you a friend of one of the party?' I asked her.

'No, I'm the wedding planner.'

'You must have had a busy couple of weeks.'

'Easiest gig ever. John paid me a lot of money and then insisted on doing everything himself.'

I heard John's voice again. Some people don't need a megaphone. 'First positions, everyone.' Ben, Mark, and the minister stood under the rose arch. The organist started playing. John made a big entrance, of course. He walked up the aisle, arm in arm with a handsome woman in her fifties, who looked like Emma thirty years on. She was obviously her mother. They were followed by Tina and two younger women in matching purple dresses. All three of them looked fabulous, but I was especially proud of Tina. She'd combed her hair down flat for the occasion. She'd been letting it grow over the past few weeks, so it was just brushing her shoulders. The dress emphasized her curves perfectly. Finally, Emma, under-dressed in a simple blouse and skirt, came in with her father.

It took a couple of run-throughs before John was happy.

He was annoyed that the music didn't always start at the right time. At one point, he even threatened to fire the organist. I didn't like John, but I couldn't help feeling sorry for him. He was taking a lot of trouble over this wedding and he'd obviously spent a huge amount of money. How would he feel if he knew what sort of marriage Ben and Emma were planning?

After the rehearsal of the ceremony, they practiced leaving the room. Even John conceded that Emma and Ben should lead them out. He and Emma's mother followed. Emma's father went out with Rebecca on one arm and Abi on the other. Obviously deeply embarrassed by any physical contact with his daughter's friends, he shook them off as soon as possible. Then came Tina with Mark. Tina looked pleased with this arrangement and perhaps squeezed Mark's arm a little too tightly. Although Mark had spent most of the rehearsal with his eyes on Emma, he looked quite happy to have another beautiful woman on his arm and sneaked a couple of covert peeks down the front of Tina's dress.

John clapped his hands and called out, 'All members of the party must be in first positions by half past three tomorrow at the latest. Is there anyone who doesn't get that? Now, you're probably hoping that I'm going to invite you all into the next room for the rehearsal dinner now. Sorry to disappoint you, but I've spent more than enough on dinner for tomorrow. You're on your own tonight.'

People started to drift away. Tina came and sat next to me. 'How was that?'

'John's missed his calling as a drill sergeant.'

'Did I look like a sad, middle-aged woman next to all those twenty-somethings?'

'No. You were the hottest woman there. No contest.'

She put her head on my shoulder. Mark walked past us and frowned, as if he resented me for being close to Tina. 'Did you see that?' she asked me. 'I think he's jealous of you.'

'He should be.'

'We'll need to have a fight tomorrow, babe. If he sees us looking too happy, he might leave us alone.'

I patted her hand. 'Okay. What do you want to do now?'

'What are my choices?'

'We're in a five-star hotel. There's a pool, a gym, a spa, two restaurants, and three bars.'

'You know what I really want to do? I'd like to grab a hot guy, go back to the room, and have some fun.'

'Mark's with Emma tonight.'

'I know.'

'Do you have anyone else in mind?'

She kissed my cheek. 'Yes. You.'

We went up to our room. I unzipped her dress and she carefully hung it up. Underneath, she was wearing a simple white bra and panties set. I sometimes think there's nothing sexier than that. She spread out in the middle of the bed. I lay down, my head level with her crotch. It wasn't like at home where I had to curl myself into a ball to lick her cunt. In this bed, I could lie on my front comfortably. Even though I knew what to expect, it was still a surprise when I peeled off her panties. It was like when a friend shaves off his beard for the first time in years. It would be a shock the next four or five times I saw it. The newly shaven skin was soft and smooth. It must have been sensitive because she giggled as I kissed it. To start with, I avoided the clit itself, licking all around it. I was starting to see why people are into shaving. I felt I could get closer to her than ever before. I explored every fold and crevice with my tongue. Then I started teasing her clit with gentle, fleeting touches. She tasted so good and the noises she was making told me how much she enjoyed it. I moved my tongue from side to side over her clit. Her moans were getting louder and closer together. Her body bucked and she put her hands on my head to stop me. 'Thank you, babe,' she said. 'Remind me to shave more often if that's what you're going to do every time.' She lay there for a moment, smiling contentedly. 'You know

I'm saving myself for Mark. But I suppose I should repay the compliment. I want you to lie back and imagine what you're going to see tomorrow. You're going to watch me being fucked by a big, strong, hairy man. If what Emma says is true, he's a bit of an animal. If he wants to get rough with me, I'm not going to object. And he's going to scratch something onto my butt. What do you think he'll write? "Slut" like he did for Emma?'

'He might go with "whore." '

'That's fine, because I'm going to be his whore *and* his slut. Actually, I want him to write "cunt." '

'You've never liked that word.'

'It depends. The place between my legs is my pussy. But I'm happy to be his cunt while he's pounding my pussy. I'm going to ride him, as well. I've been dreaming of that for weeks. You love it when I lower myself slowly onto your cock, babe. Tomorrow, I'm going to do that to him. He's going to be the first one to fuck my shaven pussy, not you. Think about that.'

She moved down the bed and wrapped her hand around the base of my cock. She licked my balls then took the whole of my cock into her warm, soft mouth. After sucking it gently, she used the tip of her tongue to tease the join between the head and the shaft. She knew that always drove me crazy. I did think about what was going to happen the next day. But if ever there was a time for living in the moment, this was it. I was lying on a king-sized bed in a five-star hotel. My beautiful, sexy wife was sucking my cock. Life couldn't get any better than this.

'Do you want to cum in my mouth?' she asked me. It seemed life *had* gotten better. She'd never let me cum in her mouth before.

'You know I do.'

'Sorry, babe. I loved the taste of Steve's cum. Kieran's is nice too. I hate yours.' That was enough to push me over the edge. She moved her head away and pointed my cock towards my bellybutton. She laughed as she made me cum all over myself.

I did a sort of limbo dance into the bathroom to stop my

cum from dripping on the carpet. After I'd cleaned myself up, we both got into bed. We lay there, watching television and chatting until it was time to go to sleep.

Chapter Thirteen

~

The next morning, we had the alarm set for six forty-five. Tina groaned when it went off and flung her head back onto the pillow. I gave her a nudge. 'Come on, you promised.'

She groaned again but got out of bed. She took a quick shower then put on jeans and a t-shirt. 'I can't believe I'm getting up at this time to teach two girls handicrafts,' she grumbled as she left the room. I rolled over and went back to sleep.

I slept for a couple of hours. Tina wasn't back when I woke up, so I luxuriated in the huge bed and watched television. She finally came in at ten past eleven. 'Some of us have been up for hours, lazy boy,' she said. She sat down on the bed and smirked. 'I've seen something you haven't.'

'What's that?'

'Emma's tits.'

'Did you take any photos?'

'In your dreams.'

'How were they?'

'Very small but kind of cute. She's young enough that they're still perky. She's got these tiny pink nipples that were made to be sucked and nibbled.' She reached under the duvet and found my cock. When she felt how hard I was, she gave it a squeeze and said, 'Forget it, babe. You're never going to see them. But you know the best thing about her tits? They were covered in cum. It looks like Mark can give Kieran a run for his money in that respect. It's doubly impressive because she said he fucked her three times. I hope he's not worn himself out. He'd better have some cum left in those balls for me. Anyway, I fanned her chest with a towel until all the cum had dried and helped her into this corset she's going to wear under her dress. Not that she needs it—skinny bitch.'

'Tina!'

'Sorry. She was really wearing it to cover up the offending area. We've doused her in Chanel so she doesn't smell like a teenage boy's pajamas. It sounds a simple idea, but getting married with another man's cum on your tits is a logistical nightmare. She wanted me to be a second pair of eyes, checking to ensure there was no trace of Mark still in the room. Then I was free to let Abi and Rebecca loose on her. She's got a busy morning. She's going to get her hair done. Then someone's coming to help her into her dress. That's the bit she's worried about. Then she's having photos taken in the grounds.'

'How did things go with Abi and Rebecca?'

'Fine. A couple of times while we were making the headdress, they said, "I'll phone Emma and ask what she wants." I told them she trusted us and wanted it to be a surprise. I did my job. I kept them away from Emma's room. She texted me at ten to say Mark had left. I told the girls to make a second headdress, in case Emma didn't like the first one. Then I went up to see how Emma was doing. She's excited. She's genuinely looking forward to the wedding, but it also sounds like she had a great night with Mark. He made her cum twice last night and again this morning. He gave her an evil-looking purple love bite on her inner thigh. And he scratched "married whore" on her ass.

She was hoping it wouldn't fade before Ben sees it tonight. Do you think he's going to scratch that on *my* ass, babe?'

'He might do.'

'After all, it's what I am. I'm *your* married whore.'

My cock was straining against my pajama bottoms. I pulled her towards me and kissed her. I was desperate to fuck her, but she pushed me away. 'We've got to get ready,' she said.

THE WEDDING CEREMONY WAS touching. A tear ran down Emma's cheek as Ben looked into her eyes and promised to love and cherish her until death did them part. When the minister pronounced them man and wife, they kissed passionately. They were in love, no doubt about it.

Afterwards, we were herded out to the garden, where we were yelled at alternately by John and a camp photographer. John wanted Ben and himself in all the photos. 'It's Ben's day as much as Emma's, and who's paying the goddamn bill?' But the photographer had fallen in love with Emma. Most of the photos he took were of her by herself or with Tina, Abi, and Rebecca.

'Be fabulous!' he shouted at them. 'The camera loves you so love it back!'

We filed into the main hall, where people were waiting with trays of champagne. Other members of the crimson suit brigade had copies of the seating plan and directed us to our places. Tina was on the top table. I was stuck on table fifteen between two women in their sixties who looked like someone's aunts. One had implausibly black hair; the other was a natural gray. They were both enjoying the free champagne and they took a shine to me. 'Putting us at a table with a good-looking single man!' said the black haired one.

'I'm not single. I'm with—'

They weren't listening. 'We'll have to take turns with him,' said the other one.

It wasn't just me they were interested in. Our waiter was a

big man with dark hair. The first aunt squealed with delight as he put the soup in front of her. 'He's got hairy wrists! I bet you're hairy all over.'

The waiter was used to flirting for tips. 'You would think the Abominable Snowman was loose, if you saw me naked.'

'Is that a promise?' shouted the second aunt.

'I'll fight you for him!' screamed the first one.

'Ladies, ladies,' said the waiter. 'Don't fight. There's more than enough for two.'

This made them cackle with delight. When he wasn't at the table, I was the center of attention. Despite my protestations that I was married, the gray-haired one kept saying I should meet her granddaughter. 'She's obsessed with horses, like you.'

'I'm not—' I began.

'She works in finance, like you.'

'I don't—'

I was glad when the waiter came over with the main course. 'Hey-la, hey-la, my boyfriend's back!' sang the aunts. He grinned and poured them more champagne.

I looked over at Tina, who was sitting next to Mark. They were chatting. To distract myself from the aunts, I wondered what they were talking about. Maybe she was telling him, 'I'm going to be your whore tonight. I'll do everything you want and you can cum wherever you like.' I could feel the bulge in my suit trousers growing again. I hoped we wouldn't have to stand up and drink a toast any time soon. I calmed myself down by reflecting that their conversation was probably the stilted sort most strangers have at weddings: 'The weather is inclement for this time of year, is it not?'

I looked at the other people on the top table. Emma was stunning in an ivory linen dress with white lace sleeves. Not surprisingly, she'd chosen a dress that covered her chest with only a shallow scoop at her throat. The floral headdress Abi and Rebecca had made for her was beautiful—small pink roses interspersed with daisies. Ben was wearing a dark blue suit with tan waistcoat and tie.

The meal was excellent, starting with butternut squash soup followed by oysters. The main course was braised short rib with asparagus and horseradish mashed potato. Dessert was a bitter chocolate crème brulée with fresh berries. Both the aunts said, 'I'll never be able to eat all this,' and then cleaned their plates.

It was half past eight by the time we finished. After the dessert plates had been cleared away, John tapped on a microphone. 'Ladies and gentlemen, I hope you've all enjoyed this marvelous dinner.' Everyone applauded. 'You'll be hearing more from me later.' He paused as if he expected spontaneous cheering at that news. When he didn't get it, he carried on, 'First, I'm going to hand over to Emma's father, Roger.'

I think Roger would have given whatever money he had left to avoid making this speech. 'Thank you to John for organizing everything. I'd like to welcome Ben to the family. And well … there it is.'

He sat down and got a pretty good round of applause. It may not have been the best speech ever, but it was short. That was a quality the people admired.

Then John stood up and spoke for twenty minutes. It would have been a good presentation to a room full of potential investors. He spoke about how well his company was doing, how much they had expanded over the last ten years, and what his plans were for the next ten years. It was a testament to the force of his personality that everyone kept listening to the end. He just about managed to make the last part of his speech relevant when he talked about how pleased he was to have Ben working with him.

Ben looked like he was about to cry as he stood up. 'I'd like to thank Roger and Annette for bringing this perfect girl into the world. Most of all, I want to thank my dad for everything. I couldn't even think about getting married if it weren't for all he's done. He's worked so hard to make today a success.' Emma stood up, went over to John and kissed him on the cheek. Ben finished by saying, 'Today is like a dream. But I'm not worried that I'm going to wake up. I'm worried Emma's going to wake up and realize what a terrible mistake she's made. In case she doesn't, I'm going to do whatever I can to make her happy. If that means doing things that husbands don't normally do, that's fine with me.'

He sat down and everyone clapped.

Ben looked worried as Mark stood up, but all Mark said was, 'I've known Ben since we were kids. He never had a big brother, so I tried to step into that role. I beat him up and stole all his toys.' Ben blushed but everyone else laughed. Mark looked at Ben and Emma and said, 'I hope to continue in the same way now you're married.'

Emma made the final speech. 'The bride speaks. The horror. My husband and I,' she paused while everyone clapped, 'would like to thank you for coming and for the lovely presents. Thank you to Tina, Rebecca, and Abi. I think you'll agree they all look fantastic. I must also thank Mark, Ben's best man. I haven't known him for long, but we've got quite close in that time. There's a sense in which he's *my* best man too.' She put a hand to her chest. 'There's a piece of him right here.' Mark smirked. Ben went scarlet. I looked at Tina. She looked back at me with a quiet smile.

By the time the speeches were finished, it was half past nine. I could see a lot of people flagging, but the party was just about to start. Emma took Ben's arm and led him into the next room. We all followed. The guests formed a circle around the dance floor as the band started playing, "You To Me Are Everything." Ben and Emma had obviously been practicing, for they flowed round the dance floor in perfect unison, gazing into each other's eyes the whole time. The song finished. They kissed.

The band played another song. Some people danced. Others went into the casino room, where the waistcoated croupiers were standing behind the tables. I hadn't seen Tina since we'd left the dining room. But I heard her voice behind me. 'Don't turn around, babe. Get us a drink. I'll find a table. Don't be surprised if I ignore you.'

I went to the bar. 'Two white wines, please,' I said.

'Certainly, sir,' said the barman.

'How much is that?'

He gave me the same look that the waiter in L'Oie Qui Fume had given me. 'It's a free bar, sir.'

'In that case, can I change my order? Could I have a bottle of champagne and two glasses?'

'Of course,' he said, but I could tell he was thinking it was a waste of good champagne, giving it to someone like me.

I went back to our table. When Tina saw the bottle, she raised her eyebrows but pointedly wasn't smiling. 'You didn't tell me we'd won the lottery.'

'John's picking up the tab,' I said, pouring. She took her glass and turned away from me. 'What do you want me to do?' I asked her.

'Look around the room. Check out the girls.' The dance floor was full of beautiful women in exquisite dresses, so this wasn't a big hardship. 'I told Mark I'm sick of you neglecting me, both emotionally and sexually.' She crossed her right leg over her left and bounced it up and down in a frustrated way. 'And now you've got eyes for any girl except me. You don't appreciate what you've got.'

'I must be insane.'

I admired the other women. Tina sat there, looking annoyed. I couldn't see Mark, so I didn't know if he was watching our show. Someone noticed us, though. 'Don't I deserve a smile after everything I've done?' It was John.

'Sorry, it's all great. It's just …' She gave me a sideways look, but didn't say anymore.

'What are your plans for the rest of the evening?' he asked. 'Are you going to dance or maybe try your luck in the casino?'

'I'm definitely going to try my luck,' said Tina.

The band started playing a jazzy tune I didn't recognize, but John said, 'This is my favorite song.' He held out his hand to Tina. 'Would you do me the honor?' He led her onto the dance floor, put his arm around her waist and held her close. He was slow dancing with her even though the tune was fast paced. She looked over John's shoulder and saw Mark watching her from the bar.

The tune finished. She excused herself, despite John's obvious disappointment, and walked back towards our table. As she approached, her face hardened. 'Right, babe, let's do it,' she said, wagging an accusing finger at me. 'Look like you're mad at me.'

I angrily pointed to the seat next to mine like I was ordering her to sit down immediately and stop embarrassing me.

'Nice,' she said, giving me a look of pure hatred. She picked up her glass. 'Shame to waste this stuff. Are you ready to flounce?'

'Yes.'

'Go back to the bedroom. Hide in the closet with the camcorder running. I'll be up as soon as I can.'

'Okay.'

'I love you,' she said, as she threw a glass of champagne in my face.

'I love you too,' I replied, as I wiped my face, gave her a murderous look, and stormed out of the room.

Chapter Fourteen

~

MY WATCH READ A little after ten. I didn't know how much time I had. There were a couple of things I wanted to do before I installed myself in the closet. I went to the bathroom downstairs. If Mark was a real stud, he might keep going for a long time. If he was about to pleasure my wife for several hours, I didn't want to watch with a full bladder. I also stopped by the dining room and picked up a bottle of water from one of the tables. I didn't want to get thirsty, either.

Back in the bedroom, I switched on the light, entered the closet, and sat down on the chair. I took the top off the bottle of water and put it down beside me. By using a coat hanger, I could keep the closet door open enough that I could point the lens of the camera through it. Looking through the viewfinder, I could see the bed was perfectly framed. I had a roll of masking tape in my pocket. I tore off a small piece and stuck it over the red recording light on the camera. Finally I went out into the room and switched off the light. Finding my way back by the glow of my phone, I sat down in the closet again. I turned the camera off. I didn't want the battery to run out at a crucial moment.

I waited. I had no idea how long it would take. From what Emma had said, Mark didn't sound like a guy who liked to linger over the seduction. There probably wouldn't be hours of erotically charged conversation in the bar. Once he had the green light, he'd want to get started as soon as possible.

Half an hour later, I heard the bottom of the door brush against the carpet. The light went on. I timed switching on the camera so it was masked by the noise of Tina closing the door. I looked through the viewfinder. Tina walked into the frame, followed by Mark. He had that smug look of a man who knows he's going to get laid. He was surprised when she reached for the television control.

'I didn't think we were here to watch TV,' he said.

'I fuck to music,' she replied. This was a good idea. I was sitting as still as possible, but there was always a danger my chair would creak and give me away. 'I need to use the bathroom. Back in a minute.' She disappeared from view. I didn't know what she was doing. And I didn't like it. Suddenly, I was tense. Maybe Mark was the type who liked to wander around opening drawers and looking into closets when he was left alone in a room. Fortunately, he just took his jacket off and lay on the bed, watching the television. When she came back, he gazed at her, open-mouthed. She was wearing a black sports-style bra, black hipster panties, black stockings and suspenders with white high heels and a black necklace. 'I thought you might like this outfit.'

He stood up, grabbed her, and kissed her. It was an aggressive kiss. He pushed his tongue deep into her mouth. She'd forgotten her resolution not to let studs kiss her on the lips. She opened her mouth wide and pushed her tongue back against his. When he drew his head back, her eyes were closed. Her lips were parted. She was a little unsteady on her feet.

'Was this bra expensive?' he asked her.

'My husband bought it for me,' she said in a low, thrilling voice. 'It cost a fortune.'

He grabbed it with both hands and pulled, splitting it down the middle. She moaned with desire. He saw my wife's breasts for the first time. Bending down, he took her left nipple into his mouth and sucked it hard. She winced as she felt his teeth on it. But she didn't want him to stop. Her hand was on the back of his head, holding it in place. When he straightened up, she took off his tie and unbuttoned his shirt. She purred with pleasure as she pushed the shirt off his broad shoulders and saw his chest for the first time. It was covered in thick dark hairs. She ran her hands through them. She kissed his chest all over and showed she could give as good as she got when she gently bit his left nipple. He reached around to stroke her ass. Then he put his hand inside her panties and felt her cunt. 'You shaved,' he said, hoarsely.

'Yeah,' she said. 'You're hairy. I'm smooth. Opposites attract.'

He moved his hand down. She opened her legs so that he could put a finger inside her. 'You're soaking, you dirty little bitch,' he said. It seemed to me he'd used that line before somewhere.

She put her hand on the bulge in his suit trousers. 'We have a hard cock and a wet pussy. What do you suggest we do?'

He laid her down on the bed and started to undo his trousers. As she watched him undress, she put her hand down her panties and touched herself. He stepped out of his trousers to reveal legs also covered in thick hairs. Tucking his thumbs in the waistband of his shorts, he was on the point of pulling them down.

And then his phone rang.

I could not believe there was a man in the world who would take a call while Tina was lying on the bed waiting for him. But he reached into his jacket pocket and took out his phone. 'Excuse me,' he said. Tina's mouth was open. She couldn't believe it either. 'How's it going?' he said into the phone. He was silent for a moment then he laughed. 'Well, I can't say I'm too surprised. Sure, I'll be right there. See you in a minute.'

Tina's expression changed from surprise to astonishment. Mark put the phone back in his pocket. 'That was Emma,' he said. 'Ben has … well, let's just say Emma needs something. I have to go to her. Sorry about that, Tina, but I'm sure you understand. After all, it is her day.'

'You're not leaving?' said Tina.

'I've got to. Emma needs me.'

'But … I can do it better!' she blurted. 'You're not even that into Emma. You made her wait while you played golf and had a drink.'

'You know about that?'

'I know everything.'

'Okay, well … I wrote something—'

'You wrote "married whore" on Emma's ass. I told you; I know everything. Why do you think I'm wearing this outfit?'

Mark shrugged as if he didn't care. 'Ben came the second he saw what I wrote. Needless to say, Emma's not satisfied.'

Tina sat up and pushed her chest forward in a last-ditch attempt. 'But my tits are bigger than hers. You said you liked them bigger.'

He nodded, maybe in agreement, but then shrugged again. 'Even so …' he said. 'And by the way, I'm seriously into Emma— even more now she's married to my best friend. Making her wait was just a way of keeping her interested.'

'It obviously worked,' she said. She pointed angrily at the door. 'All right, go.'

He put his clothes on, picked up his jacket, and went out.

When the door shut behind him, I sat with her on the bed and put my arms around her. She was shaking. 'That was the most humiliating thing that's ever happened to me,' she said.

'He's an idiot,' I said.

'Can you believe anyone would leave me for Emma? I could do so much more for him than that cunt ever could.'

'Tina. She's your friend.'

She calmed down a little. 'Yes, she is. I suppose he's right in a way. It is her wedding night. She deserves to have good sex, and if her husband can't satisfy her ….' She paused and looked at me. 'You lasted about ten seconds on our wedding night. I didn't send out for reinforcements.'

'I licked you for over an hour and made you cum three times.'

'Yes, you did. I went to sleep satisfied.'

'Do you want me to lick you now?'

'No, I need cock.' I moved in to kiss her but she pushed me away. 'Sorry, Rob, not yours.' She stood up and saw herself in the mirror—standing there in panties and a ripped bra. 'I'm so glad he liked my outfit,' she said bitterly, as she pulled the bra off and stuffed it into the wastepaper basket. 'I can't believe I shaved my pussy for that guy.'

She went into the bathroom and came back with her dress on. I zipped her up as she said, 'You get back into the closet. I'm going to see if John fancies another dance.'

'*John?*'

'I know he's a bit old but he must have learnt a few things in all those years. Let's give him a day in court.'

'He hates anything to do with infidelity.'

She made a face. 'I don't buy that. He was getting excited when I was dancing with him. I reckon he's like a politician who talks about family values while he's snorting coke from a hooker's cleavage.'

She left the room and I went back to my seat in the closet. I couldn't believe what had happened. I'd been looking forward to watching Mark fuck her. I'd been intrigued to see if he was better than Steve. But now I was looking forward to seeing her with John. I imagined him barking out crisp orders. 'Strip! On your knees! Suck!' Or possibly he was one of those men who was dominant everywhere except the bedroom. Maybe he'd kiss Tina's feet and say, 'Punish me if I fail to satisfy you, mistress.'

The door opened and Tina came in, followed by a man. It wasn't John. It was the waiter who'd served at my table during dinner. The two aunts would be disappointed. They wouldn't be the ones seeing him naked tonight. 'Did you notice me in the wedding party?' Tina asked him, as she closed the door.

'Of course I did. You're beautiful in that dress.'

She took off her dress with a minimum of fuss and stood in front of him in her panties. 'What about out of it?'

'Is that all you've had on under your dress all day?' he asked.

'Oh yes,' she said. 'I wanted to be ready in case I met a man like you.'

He looked confused. 'Aren't you married?'

'Don't worry about my husband. He's downstairs in the casino, losing. He'll crawl back here when he's lost everything. If he gets in our way, we'll tell him to fuck off.'

'You're bad.'

'You have no idea.' She took off the panties and let him gaze at her naked body.

He looked down at her cunt. 'I notice you—' he began.

'I always keep it like this,' she lied. 'I don't want anything getting between my pussy and that big hard cock of yours.'

I thought she might have been tempting fate. She still had no evidence that his cock was either big or hard.

He kissed her. He didn't have the confidence Mark had. It was a more tentative kiss. She soon put him at ease. She started undressing him. Knowing he probably had to return the uniform at the end of his shift, she didn't rip anything. She took off his jacket and put it on the chair. She unbuttoned his shirt. If she'd been trying to find a replacement for Mark, she'd done well. Their bodies were remarkably similar. The same powerful but not obsessively toned frame. The same covering of dark hair. Even the hair on their heads was almost identical. The only real differences were in their features. The waiter had a larger nose and bushier eyebrows.

'I love a man with a hairy chest,' she said. 'Men with hairless chests aren't real men.' She was saying this for me. I was glad she was making me a part of it. She kissed his chest and stomach all over. Then she flicked his nipple with the tip of her tongue. She did this at such an angle that I and the camera could see it perfectly.

She knelt down to undo his belt while he took his shirt off and threw it onto the chair. When she pulled down his trousers and shorts, I saw that I needn't have worried that she was tempting fate. His cock was long, thick, and fully erect. She ran her tongue around its head, then put her lips around it and started sucking. He thrust his hips forward to get his cock deeper inside her mouth.

She stood up. Wrapping her hand around his cock, she led him to the bed. She'd put a new pack of condoms in the bedside table drawer. She'd never gotten round to opening them with Mark, so there was a short delay while she peeled off the cellophane. She took a condom out of the box and put it on him. She lay down on the bed, and he got on top of her. He tried to kiss her and stroke her breasts, but she wasn't interested in foreplay. Taking his cock in her hand, she slid it inside her. 'Kiss my neck while you're fucking me,' she said. 'I love that.' I guessed she had an ulterior motive in asking that. She didn't want to look at his face. She rubbed her hands over his hairy body as he started to fuck her. Looking at me, she silently mouthed, 'Mark … oh, Mark.'

She'd been looking forward to riding Mark's cock, so I wasn't surprised when she said, 'You lie down now.' He lay on his back. Tina turned to face me. She was going to do the reverse cowgirl on him. As she lowered her cunt towards his cock, she gave me her wicked look. She was going to do to him what she hadn't done to me the day before. She felt her cunt around his shaft again. She moved up and down slowly, enjoying the feel of his full length inside her. I loved the contrast of her completely smooth cunt sliding down towards a dense bush of dark hair. 'How you doing back there?' she asked over her shoulder.

'I'm enjoying the view,' he said. 'Your butt is awesome.'

'Best butt at the wedding?' He didn't answer, so she asked, 'Am I better than the bride?'

'I don't know. I've never had the bride.'

This was no time to worry about little things like facts. 'Am I better than the bride?' she asked, again.

'You're both beautiful women,' he said.

This was completely the wrong thing to say. She mouthed, 'Oh, for fuck's sake,' at me.

She was annoyed, but not enough to stop. She managed to rotate her body so she was facing him without breaking contact. She spent a long time riding him. He had staying power. She grabbed her breasts. As she squeezed her nipples, her body juddered uncontrollably and she cried out. After a moment's pause, she looked at him. 'Is it okay if I go again?' she asked. 'I've had a hard day.'

'Go for it,' he said.

She put her hand between her legs. I couldn't see exactly what she was doing, but I knew she was rubbing her clit as she carried on riding his cock. Her second orgasm was quieter. Her moan as she came was one of satisfaction rather than ecstasy.

Lifting herself off him, she knelt on the bed and took the condom off his cock. She held up her left hand. 'You see this?' she said. 'What is it?'

'Your wedding ring,' he replied.

'The symbol of the bond between me and my husband. It's special. Sacred, you might say. So it would be terrible if I let another man cum all over it. That would make me the sluttiest wife ever.'

I had trouble keeping my breathing quiet as he jerked his cock with her right hand and held the left under it, ready to catch his cum. It wasn't long until he emptied his balls into my wife's hand. He lifted his head so he could watch her carefully rubbing his cum into every part of her wedding ring. 'You're *very* bad,' was all he could say.

She gave him a moment to get his breath back, then said, 'If you go back to the party now, maybe no one will have missed you.'

I looked at my watch and was surprised to see it was a quarter to midnight. He'd been here over an hour. That was a long break for a waiter to take during a shift.

'You're worth getting fired for,' he said and kissed her on the lips. He put his uniform back on and went out.

She shut the door behind him. I opened the closet and stepped out. I couldn't believe what I'd just seen. My heart was pounding and I desperately wanted to fuck her. I wasn't sure if I wanted to cum inside her or cum over her wedding ring myself. Having two men's cum on her wedding ring would make her even sluttier. I was also thinking I might lick his cum off the wedding ring. I was sure she'd love that. Then I saw her face. She was crying. Rob the horny cuckold immediately gave way to Rob the caring husband. I put my arm around her. 'Hey, what's wrong?'

'Nothing,' she said, unconvincingly. 'Is there a minibar in here?'

'This is a classy place. It has a drinks cabinet.'

She went over to the cabinet and came back with two glasses and a bottle of fifteen-year-old Bowmore Scotch. She handed me the bottle and held the glasses out in front of her.

'Pour me a quadruple.'

'I thought you didn't like whiskey.'

'This is an emergency.' I poured us each a large measure and we sat on the bed together. 'And this stuff is good,' she said, after her first mouthful.

'We'd better not get used to this. Tomorrow, we have to go back to the real world, where staying at a Holiday Inn is the height of luxury.' She didn't say anything. She kept on sipping her drink. A tear ran down her cheek. 'Talk to me, my love,' I said.

'I suppose it's a natural part of life,' she said. 'Someone always comes along who's younger and more interesting. I'm Madonna and Emma is Lady Gaga.'

'I'd still choose Madonna.'

'Probably not a decision you'll ever have to make, Rob. But I've got to face it. I'm not the hottest wife in town anymore.'

'You're still the only one for me.'

'I know, babe, but what does a hot wife do when she can't attract people anymore?'

'What are you talking about? It took you less than ten minutes to find that guy.'

'I was supposed to be having sex with the best man tonight. I ended up fucking one of the waiters. Talk about a downgrade.'

'You came twice!'

'I know. As a fuck, it was good. Even he'd rather have been with Emma.'

'He didn't say that.'

'It's what he meant. I'm not the Queen Bee anymore.'

I touched the tip of her nose affectionately. 'Don't abdicate because one drone flew out of your hive.'

'It's not just one. I haven't spoken to Kieran in weeks.'

'That's what you wanted.'

'But *he* shouldn't want it. Not seeing me should be killing him. Has he tried to contact me?'

'He hasn't started stalking you, the way Steve did. That's a good thing.'

'There's nothing wrong with a *Hey, we haven't hooked up in a while—how's Wednesday looking?* message on Facebook.'

'Maybe he saw the signs and realized you were getting bored.'

'What about Steve? A few months ago, he was ready to risk his career to be with me. Now I offer it to him on a plate, and he doesn't want to know. I've lost it, babe.'

'I love you and I hate him but—'

'But what?'

'His affair with you did end up with his boss finding out.'

She gave me a look. 'Whose fault was that?'

'I did what I had to do.' At the time, I'd been the hero for saving her job. Was she really making me out to be the bad guy now? 'You can see why he wouldn't want to get involved again.'

She paused and looked sulky. 'You might be right. But what about Adam? The first words out of his mouth when he saw me were "I have no interest in having sex with you." '

'And what about John? The first thing he said was that we'd have to ugly you up or you'd outshine Emma on her wedding day.'

'He's the type who turns on the charm when he wants to. I'm sure he says things like that to every woman he meets.'

'There were hundreds of women at that reception. Who was the first one he wanted to dance with?'

She smiled. 'True. Maybe I've still got it.'

'Of course you have. By the way, what happened to John? You said you were going to come back with him.'

'He was having a good run on the crap table. He didn't even notice me.'

'Do you want to go downstairs and join the party now?'

'I'd rather go to bed.'

'That's fine.'

'I want to sleep with my husband's arms around me.'

'I'm sure that can be arranged.'

'I love you, Rob.'

'I love you, Tina. You've still got another man's cum on your wedding ring.'

Chapter Fifteen

~

WE DROVE HOME AFTER breakfast the next morning. It was good to see Boris again. And he was certainly pleased to see us. When Louise opened her front door, he flung himself at me. But Tina and I both felt deflated when we arrived home. Our house looked small and basic compared to the hotel. We didn't have a team of cleaners coming in every morning to spruce the place up. Our couch was covered in dust and dog hairs. 'Why aren't you rich?' asked Tina, as she sat down and looked round the den. 'I should have seduced John. He'd have kept me in the style to which I've become accustomed.'

I sat down next to her. 'Instead, you're a quiet smile that the waiter's girlfriend doesn't understand.'

Her arms were folded across her chest. 'Did you film me with the waiter? Or did you switch off when Mark left?'

'I got it all.'

'We must watch it sometime. With the director's commentary.'

'I think the leading lady's commentary might be more interesting. We can watch it this evening, if you like.'

She unfolded her arms. 'Actually, babe, I'm more in the mood to *make* a movie tonight.'

'And your co-star will be …?'

She lowered her eyes and looked almost embarrassed as she said, 'Kieran.'

'I thought—'

'I know, but after the ups and downs of the last couple of days, I want something boring and dependable—with a huge cock.'

'I wonder what he'll say when he sees you've shaved.'

' "Not my scene," ' we said together.

'I'll send him a message,' she said.

WE DID END UP watching the film of Tina and the waiter that night. Kieran didn't reply to her message. She was in a funk. 'Even my fallback stud isn't interested in me anymore.' So I skipped over the part where Mark left her and started the film when the waiter arrived. While we were watching, I told her how great she looked and impressed upon her how much the waiter was into her. We stopped the film halfway through and went upstairs to make love.

A WEEK LATER, TINA was on her laptop, checking her emails. 'Still nothing from Kieran,' she called out.

'It's his loss,' I said from the next room.

'But Adam asks if he can come round on Saturday.'

'I'll hide all my best shirts.'

Then she said, 'You'll definitely want to see this, babe.'

I was watching television with Boris on my knee. 'Can I look at it later?'

'It's Emma porn,' she said. I pointed at the floor. Boris wasn't happy, but he jumped down. I went into the dining room. 'I thought that would get you,' said Tina, sourly. 'Read that.' I looked over her shoulder. 'Tell me when you want me to scroll down.'

Dear Tina and Rob,

The sun is shining. I'm sitting beside the most amazing crystal clear turquoise lagoon. I'm drinking a cocktail of rum, amaretto and cranberry juice. I don't know what it's called but it's scrummy.

'"It's a hard-knock life …"' I sang.
'I've definitely got to find me a rich man,' said Tina.

We arrived in the Maldives on Sunday evening. I slept late the first morning. I was knackered after the wedding and the flight. I half woke up when Ben left the room. I thought he was going off for an early morning swim, so I turned over and went to sleep again. He was back in bed next to me when I woke up properly. 'Good morning,' he said. 'How do you feel?'

I snuggled into him. 'Tired but happy. You?'

'I'm on honeymoon with the most wonderful girl in the world. How do you think I feel? I never gave you your wedding present, did I?'

'Being married to you is enough.' I reached into his shorts and put my hand around his prick. I told myself that size didn't matter. It belonged to the man I loved.

'Let me go and change,' he said.

He went into the bathroom and closed the door. I propped myself up on the pillows, curious to see what was going to happen next. Ben had fantasized about role-playing before. But I'd always been the one dressing up. He'd talked about buying me a stern headmistress outfit or a sexy air hostess uniform. I wondered what he'd chosen for himself. I hoped he wasn't going to come out in a Batman costume that would just make me squeal with laughter. The bathroom door opened and I saw what he'd changed into. He'd changed into Mark.

Mark was naked in the bathroom doorway. He looked like an animal—strong and powerful. I was too surprised and turned on to say anything. I swept away the bedclothes so he could see my naked body. He sprang across the room and landed on the bed. He kissed me. I placed my left hand around his prick. It felt good to have a full-sized one in my hand again. 'Is this my wedding present?' I asked Ben.

'Do you like it?'

'I love it.' I looked into Mark's eyes. 'Now that I'm an honest married woman, I hope you're going to treat me with the respect I deserve.' He didn't say anything. He grabbed my wrists and pinned them behind my head. I pretended to struggle but he was too strong for me and anyway, the last thing I wanted to do was escape. He kissed me. It was too early in the morning for him to taste of beer but I loved the feel of his rough tongue pushing into my mouth. He dug his fingers into my boobs, leaving red marks all over them. He put his lips around my left nipple and sucked it hard. Then he bit down on it. I screamed.

'Lucky bitch,' said Tina.

'He did the same to you,' I reminded her.

'Yes, but she's not about to say, "Then his phone rang and he fucked off." '

He turned me over so I was lying on my front. Pushing my legs apart, he knelt between them. He scratched my bum, but he didn't write anything. He just raked his nails down my buttocks. Ben makes love to me so gently, treating me like a dried flower that will crumble under his touch. Mark acts like I'm a lump of clay. He picks me up, throws me down, and works my body until it's the way he wants it. He lay on top of me.

His hairy chest was against my back. I felt his prick at the entrance to my cunt. I raised myself up so he could enter me more easily.

As he was screwing me from behind, he said, 'Tell me what you are.'

'I'm a whore for your prick.'

'What sort of whore are you?'

'A dirty whore. A cheap whore.'

'What sort of whore are you?' he repeated.

I realized what he wanted to hear. 'I'm a married whore.'

Hearing those words out loud was too much for both of us. I came as I felt Mark's spunk filling the condom.

Afterwards, Mark lay down beside me. I put my left arm around him. Ben had been watching everything from the bathroom doorway. I held out my right arm to him and he joined us on the bed. I felt a moment of perfect happiness. I was on my honeymoon. I'd just had great sex. I was lying in bed with my husband and my lover—the love and the lust of my life.

I needed to ask one question. 'How?'

'He flew over on the red eye,' said Ben. 'I went to the airport to pick him up while you were still asleep. You're a heavy sleeper, my angel. I managed to sneak him into the bathroom without you knowing.'

'I'm glad you did. Thank you, Ben, it's a lovely present. Better than a pair of socks any day.'

'Shall we go and have breakfast and let Mark get some sleep?'

'She doesn't say anything about Mark being with me the night of the wedding,' said Tina.

'Maybe he didn't mention it,' I said.

'A stud who's also a gentleman. Who'd have thought it?'

We carried on reading.

It was a more regular honeymoon than you might think. Mark realized that even a hot wife and a cuckold need to be alone sometimes. Mark's a mad keen swimmer, so he spent a lot of time down at the beach. We fell into a routine. We woke up late in the morning. Mark and I had sex. Then he left Ben and me alone during the day. We were like any other newlyweds. We walked along the beach holding hands. We went into town and he bought me presents. We sat in cafés and shared ice cream. In the evening, we hooked up with Mark again. We went out for dinner then went back to our room.

The evenings weren't so traditional. On the first evening he was there, Mark said, 'There's something I want to try.'

Ben immediately said, 'Uh-oh.' Experience has taught Ben that it does not always go well for him when Mark wants to try something.

Mark wanted me to be his slave. He stood in the middle of the room, fully dressed, and made me take off all my clothes and crawl towards him. I had to kneel in front of him, with my hands behind my back. He made me apologize for my breasts. I looked up into his cruel eyes and said, 'I'm sorry my breasts are too small for you. Please screw me from behind so you don't have to look at them.' Then I had to beg to be allowed to suck his prick. He refused three times, so I made my begging more desperate. I told him I didn't deserve such a magnificent penis in my mouth, but that I would do my best to please him. Finally, he got it out and I put my lips around it. He pulled my hair all the time I was sucking his prick so I wouldn't enjoy it too much. He made me stop after a minute because he said I was the worst he'd ever had. Then I had to crawl to the bed and get on it in the doggy position, making sure he couldn't see my skanky little boobs. He came up behind me and spanked my bum twice. I said, 'Thank you for spanking me. Please do it some more. I need to be taught a lesson.' But he wouldn't. He just screwed me from behind. He was trying to be selfish. He didn't want to make me cum, but I was too turned on. I came immediately. I apologized like mad for having an orgasm without permission. Then he came inside me and that was the end of the game.

I stood up. He kissed me and then we both laughed. It was fun. I'm never going to be a 24/7 slave, but I like playing at it occasionally. And I loved Ben's reaction when I told him, 'I will never let you treat me like that, but Mark can do that any time he wants.' Ben was so turned on, he could hardly breathe.

Anyway, better go. Writing this has made me all hot and bothered. I need to go and find Mark. Maybe he's thought of a new game we can play.

Love, Emma.

I finished reading. 'Are you okay?'
'Sure,' said Tina. 'Why wouldn't I be?'
'You don't wish you could be Mark's slave?'
She pulled the front of her t-shirt down so I could see her tits. 'Can you imagine me apologizing?'
'Bragging, yes. Apologizing, no.'
'Mark belongs to Emma. He's her stud. I have to accept that.'
'I must admit that reading that did—'
'Me too. Do you want to go upstairs?'
'Oh, yes.'

Chapter Sixteen

~

Three days later, we had finished eating and Boris had settled down on our laps when we heard a noise outside. Someone was coming up the drive. Boris leapt down and ran to the door. He didn't bark. His tail was wagging. 'Whoever it is, Boris likes him,' I said, getting up.

'Adam?' suggested Tina.

I went to the door and opened it. Emma and Ben were standing outside. 'Hey, guys!' I said. 'When did you get back?'

'Yesterday,' said Emma. 'We came back to a shit storm. Can we come in?'

I stood aside, and they went into the den. Tina jumped up and gave them both a hug and a kiss. 'How was the rest of your honeymoon?' she asked.

'Great,' said Emma, looking devastated. 'But that's not why we're here.' She sat on the couch next to Tina. I told Ben to take the other chair and crouched down on the floor.

'What happened?' asked Tina.

'Paige happened,' said Emma. She reached into her bag, took out her packet of cigarettes, and lit one. I raised my eyebrows at Tina. She shook her head almost imperceptibly, telling me to let it go. 'Do you know what the spiteful bitch has done?'

'What?'

'You remember I said I was going to spend my wedding night with my husband? Well, that didn't work out. Ben saw the love bite on my thigh and the words "married whore" scratched on my bum. He made a moaning noise and that was him done for the night. So I had to call Mark.'

'Did you?' asked Tina, innocently.

'I knew Paige had a room on the same floor. I didn't know she was spying on us. She saw Mark going into the bridal suite at eleven o'clock. Like the spoilt brat she is, she went running to Daddy.'

'And told him what?' I asked. 'The best man needed to see the groom on the evening of the wedding. Nothing strange about that. It could have been to return his cufflinks.'

'She had her ear pressed against the door. She heard Mark doing things that go beyond normal best man duties.'

'I see,' said Tina. She gave Emma another hug. 'It'll be embarrassing next time you see John, but—'

'It's more serious than that,' said Ben. 'He called and told me that Emma's a whore.'

'It's not so sexy when it's my father-in-law saying it,' said Emma. She looked around for an ashtray and realized her mistake. 'Oh, sorry, I should have—'

'Don't worry,' said Tina, handing her a saucer.

'He said she's not fit to be part of this family and I need to get the marriage annulled immediately,' said Ben.

'Did you explain?' I asked.

'You can't explain anything to my dad when he's worked up. Anyway, he'd never understand.'

'He can't force you to get an annulment,' Tina said.

'Well … no,' faltered Ben.

'Our flat,' said Emma. 'Who do you think owns it?'

'He also says he can't have any scandal attached to the company,' said Ben. 'If I don't get the marriage annulled, I'll be out of a job.'

'Can you really fire someone over that?' asked Tina.

Ben shrugged. 'Maybe not, but he can afford better lawyers than I can.'

'We could end up on the street,' said Emma.

'That's not going to happen,' said Tina. 'You can always stay here if necessary.'

Emma looked round the room and a tear ran down her cheek. Tina's face hardened.

'Have you actually admitted to your dad that Mark had sex with Emma on your wedding night?' I asked.

Ben shook his head. 'But that doesn't matter. He's decided.'

'How did you leave it with him?'

'He's given me a week to start seeking an annulment. I have to choose between my wife and my life.' He quickly looked over at Emma. 'Obviously I'm going to choose my wife.'

'Don't do anything yet,' I said. 'We might be able to help you.'

'How?'

'I need to discuss it with Tina.' They looked at us expectantly, waiting for us to start discussing it. 'Privately,' I added.

I could tell they were wondering what could be private after everything we'd shared, but Emma stood up and headed for the front door. 'Come on, Ben. I'm sure they know what they're doing.'

I wasn't sure we knew what we were doing. I closed the front door behind them. When I came back into the den, I flapped a dish towel around to get rid of the smoke. Tina was looking at the floor with pursed lips. 'I know what you're thinking,' she said. I found this hard to believe. 'Do we really want to help them?' she asked.

'Of course. They're our friends.'

'Yes they are. I'm thinking of what's best for Emma.'

'Honestly?'

'All her life, she's had everything dropped into her lap. She grew up with her dad lavishing everything on her. After he lost his money, she didn't waste much time finding a rich husband.

Maybe it would do her good if she had to—gasp!—work for a living.'

'Tina, it's not her fault that Mark ran out on you.'

She sighed and spread her hands in a broad gesture. 'Yes, you're right, babe. I suppose we should help them. So you want me to fuck John if he promises to let Ben and Emma off the hook?'

'What? No! I don't want you to do anything of the sort!'

'Why not? Like you said, they're our friends. Greater love hath no woman than this, that she lay herself down for her friends.'

'If my plan works, it won't come to that.'

She looked at me, intrigued. 'What is your plan?'

Chapter Seventeen

~

I PHONED JOHN'S OFFICE. I had to go through a number of gatekeepers. It helped that I kept repeating the words, 'It's about Ben.' Finally, I heard a curt voice on the other end of the line. 'John Jacobs. Who is this?'

'It's Rob Matthews.'

'Who?'

'Tina's husband.'

'Ah yes. What can I do for you?'

'Well, I've been hearing these wild rumors about Emma and Mark on the night of the wedding.'

'What do you mean, "wild rumors"? They're true.'

'No, they're not.'

'What makes you say that?'

'I have proof. If you could give me a few minutes of your time, I'll show you.'

He was quiet for a moment. 'All right. Come to my office at three.'

He hung up. 'Let me check my diary,' I said to the tone.

Fortunately, my last lesson that afternoon finished at half past two. I was able to drive to John's office and arrive at two minutes to three. 'I'm here to see John Jacobs,' I told the receptionist.

There was that look again. I was getting tired of it. It said, *You don't belong here.* 'Name?' she said. I told her. Looking at her computer screen, she reluctantly admitted that John was expecting me. She pointed me towards the elevator and told me to go up to the top floor.

I stepped out of the elevator into a labyrinth of high-powered men—they were all men—in glass-walled offices. Other, more ordinary people were sitting at desks. I asked one of these ordinary people where I could find John and saw that look again. I went along a corridor with framed pictures of cars on the walls. I knocked on the door at the end. 'Come!' he shouted. After I went in and closed the door behind me, he stood up, walked around his desk, and came over to shake my hand. He was dressed expensively but casually in a blue designer shirt with light brown chinos and a thick brown belt. Two bottles of Tasmanian Rain water sat on a side table. He poured me a glass. I tasted it, thinking that it was no different from the stuff that came out of my tap. He sat back down behind his big leather topped desk. 'Now, what's this proof you claim to have?'

'I need to give you some background first.' He didn't say anything, but looked at his watch. I spoke quickly. 'Tina and I have a slightly unusual relationship. She's a hot wife. I'm a cuckold.'

'You mean she cheats on you?' I could see what Ben had meant about his dad getting angry at any mention of infidelity. His face was red and his mouth was tight.

'We don't like the word "cheat." We prefer "share." '

He made a dismissive gesture. 'That's hairsplitting. I knew you and Tina were having problems.'

'No, we're fine.'

'It's fine for a woman to throw champagne in her husband's face at a wedding reception?'

'We have fights, like every other couple in the world. But we're happy.'

'Impossible. If one partner is cheating, that *always* means something is deeply wrong with the marriage.'

'That's why we don't say "cheating." It's not hairsplitting. It's an important distinction. We both chose to live like this. There's no deception.'

'Why on earth would you agree to that?'

'It excites me.'

He shook his head. 'I don't see it.'

I shrugged. 'There are men who like to wear ladies' underwear.'

'I don't understand that, either.'

'Nor do I. You can't argue with people's tastes.'

'Mm,' he said, as if he was only too willing to argue with people's tastes. 'Anyway, I don't see how it's relevant.'

'It's how I know Mark wasn't with Emma on the night of the wedding. He was with Tina.'

'Paige said she saw Mark going into the bridal suite at eleven o'clock. Then she heard what she describes as "intimate noises" coming from the room.'

I looked around the office. There were blinds on all the glass walls. 'Could we close the blinds?' I asked.

'Why?'

'There's something I want to show you. It's most definitely for your eyes only.'

He pressed a button on his desk. The blinds slid down smoothly over the walls and the window.

I took Tina's laptop out of my bag and put it on the desk. 'I must ask you to treat everything you see as strictly confidential. Emma and Ben know nothing about this.'

I switched on the laptop and moved my finger across the touch pad until I could click on the video clip. Our room in the hotel appeared on the screen. After a few moments of dead screen time, Tina and Mark came in. She switched on the television. My film now had a lo-fi pop soundtrack. 'You'll note that the time stamp on the screen is ten forty on the night of the wedding.' Tina walked out of frame and there were a couple of dull minutes as Mark sat on the bed and watched television.

'How did you get these pictures?' he asked.

'I was sitting in the closet, filming their encounter.'

'Mm,' he said again.

Tina came back into the shot, wearing the black bra and panties outfit. The dialogue was masked by the music. John started as he saw Mark ripping off her bra . I paused the film. 'You don't want to see the next bit,' I said. John looked like he wanted very much to see the next bit. 'You can imagine what happened after this. So the story that Mark was with Emma that night simply doesn't add up.'

Tina's left breast was visible on the screen. I hoped that would cloud John's judgement. But you don't get to be a captain of industry if you're distracted by a breast. 'That was at ten forty-six. Paige saw him go into the bridal suite fourteen minutes later.'

'He finished with the matron of honor and moved on to the bride a quarter of an hour later? Who is this guy? Super Stud?'

'He's a vigorous young man. It wouldn't be impossible.'

'All right, if you need more proof ….' I put my finger back on the touch pad. I tried to make it look like I was choosing part of the film at random. In fact, I'd made my scene selection carefully.

The screen showed Tina lying on her back on the bed. A dark-haired man was fucking her. He was kissing her neck, so his face was hidden. And the focus was on his hairy butt thrusting in and out. I was glad we didn't have a better camera. It was the waiter, but when filmed from behind, he looked exactly like Mark. 'Look at the time stamp. Ten past eleven. The time when he was supposed to be in the bridal suite.'

I selected a later part of the film. The waiter was on his back now. Tina was riding him in the reverse cowgirl position. Her breasts were bouncing as she moved up and down on his cock. Her eyes were closed and her head thrown back. His face was hidden behind her body. I only played that clip for a couple of seconds. Tina was about to sway to the side and show the waiter's face. 'That was at twenty to midnight.'

I switched off the laptop and closed the lid before he could ask to see more. He sat back in his chair, breathing heavily. Tina was right. However much he disapproved of infidelity, he'd enjoyed watching it. But he was still trying to think straight. He touched his index fingers to his lips. 'Why would Paige lie?'

I shrugged. 'You know her a lot better than I do. I get the feeling she's jealous.'

'Of what?'

'Maybe she felt Ben's wedding was more lavish than hers.'

'That's not true. I spent exactly the same on hers—when you take inflation into account.'

I gave him a searching look. 'People in the throes of jealousy don't take inflation into account.'

'You think she'd make this up to get back at Ben?'

'Sibling rivalry is a terrible thing,' I said, shaking my head.

'I won't have people lying to me,' he said, his face reddening again.

I hadn't thought of that. From the few minutes I'd spent with her, I hadn't seen much to like about Paige. Squealing to her dad had been a bitchy thing to do. But I didn't want her to suffer the full force of her father's rage for telling the truth. For all I knew, she relied on him financially as much as Ben did. 'This might be a good time to show her how much you love her,' I said gently.

His look said that if he wanted my family counseling, he'd ask for it. Then his face softened. 'Well, I'm much obliged to you for coming forward with this information. It can't have been easy for you.I don't claim to respect your lifestyle and I'm not at all happy that my son's wedding was used as the arena for such goings on. I *do* respect you for wanting to protect him.'

He shook my hand and pressed the button to raise the blinds. I took the elevator to the ground floor and walked out of the building. When I was outside, I phoned Tina at work. 'Success?' she asked me.

'I think he bought it,' I said, proudly.

'Super Cuck saves the day once again.'

Chapter Eighteen

~

ON Saturday afternoon at four o'clock, the doorbell rang. Boris barked just once and wagged his tail, again just once. That meant it was the postman—late as usual. Boris didn't like the postman, but tolerated him because we seemed to enjoy getting letters. It was a special delivery for Tina of a shallow box, two feet long by a foot and a half wide. We sat down in the den as she opened it. Inside was her copy of Emma and Ben's wedding album. The first page showed Ben shaking hands with his dad. On the second page, they were standing with Mark at the main entrance of the hotel. Then there were ten glossy shots of Emma posing in her wedding dress. These were followed by the photos taken after the ceremony. Tina was in six of them. I was only in one. Tina liked the way she looked in the photos.

We were still poring over the pictures when there was another ring at the door. This time, Boris curvetted with excitement. That meant it was someone he liked—probably someone with chicken.

I opened the door and Adam came in. He put down his bag and shook hands with me. Then he kissed Tina on the cheek and gave Boris a chicken fillet. 'What are you looking at?' he asked.

'Wedding photos,' said Tina.

The album was open at a photo of Emma posing with Tina, Abi, and Rebecca. 'You look great,' said Adam.

'Thank you,' she replied. 'What do you think of Emma?'

'It's a nice dress,' he said, blandly.

'All eyes were on her.'

'That's only natural on her wedding day.' Adam turned back to the second page and saw John, Ben, and Mark. He pointed at Mark. 'That's the man you were after.'

'Well spotted,' I said.

'He's definitely your type.'

'If only I was his,' she said, puffing out her cheeks.

'It didn't work out well?'

Tina explained what had happened on the night of the wedding. Her eyes were downcast as she described Mark answering Emma's call and leaving. She didn't see Adam stepping forward. She only realized something was happening when he kissed her assertively on the lips. Her eyes widened. She had not expected that. Then there was doubt in her eyes. She had thought about this moment. Now she was working out how she felt about it actually happening. That took her only a second. She put her arms around his neck and kissed him back.

We went up to the bedroom. Boris watched us go. He's learnt that, if we go upstairs with another man, there's no point in following us.

The three of us went into the bedroom and turned on the light. Tina was wearing her old Betty Boop t-shirt. 'Do you want me to put on something sexier?' she asked. 'I wear this when I'm slobbing round the house.' She gave him her wicked look. 'But I'm very fond of it. I've had it for years.'

The t-shirt was doomed from that moment. He grabbed it and ripped it. It fell to the floor. She reached behind her back to undo her bra. He shook his head. 'Leave it on.'

I went to my position by the side of the bed while he undressed. I can honestly say his body wasn't any better than mine. But I'd be happy if I still looked like that at his age. He obviously spent a few hours in the gym every week and was careful about what he ate. There wasn't much definition in his abs, but he'd managed to stave off middle-aged spread. He had a thin covering of hair on his chest and belly, most of it still dark. His cock was a little longer than mine, but about the same thickness. His pubes were dark, with a sprinkling of gray.

He positioned her on all fours on the bed. I knew he was going to choose this position. The fantasy she'd shared with him left no doubt that this was what she wanted.

What he did next was more unexpected. He picked up the bottle of baby oil from her bedside table and unscrewed the cap. He squeezed half the oil into the cleavage of her buttocks. After drizzling more over his cock, he put the bottle down. He parted her buttocks. Her asshole was already shiny, but he carefully massaged the oil into it. Nudging up against it with the tip of his cock, he said, 'Yes?'

'Yes,' said Tina, strongly but with a hint of nervousness in her voice. She braced herself on the bed. She hadn't been fucked up the ass since Steve had taken her over the dining room table.

Adam's cock wasn't like Steve's, but the head looked big next to my wife's tight little asshole. He used his hands to keep her buttocks spread as he slowly pushed himself into her. He could tell she hadn't done this for a while, so he moved slowly, giving her time to get used to it again. 'Oh, yeah,' she moaned with every thrust. Then she said, 'My pussy's not good enough for you?'

'It's too big,' he said.

'It's been stretched by Kieran's cock. I wouldn't even feel you in there.'

'You can feel me in your ass, though.'

'Only just.' He thrust into her harder. 'Oh yes!' she said. 'Don't hold back. Fuck me like you hate me.'

'I do hate you,' he said.

'Show me how much.'

He dug the nail of his right index finger into her left buttock and started scratching a word into her skin. 'You bastard,' she said, biting her bottom lip in pain while moaning with desire. After he'd finished, she asked breathlessly, 'What did you write?'

'Rob, tell her,' he said.

I couldn't read it from where I was so I walked round and stood beside him. Standing so close, I was aware of his manly scent. He had picked up on her desire for that, as well. He didn't smell bad. He just hadn't overdone the soap or the cologne. He smelled the way she'd hoped Mark would smell. 'What does it say, babe?' she asked.

'You don't want to know.'

'Does it say "slut"?'

'No.'

' "Cunt"?'

'Worse.'

'Worse than "cunt"? Tell me.'

'It says "Emma." '

Tina gave a strangled cry. 'Do you wish I was Emma?'

'You know I do,' he said.

'Is she better than me?'

'She's so much hotter, sexier … and younger than you.'

'I'm an old slut compared to her.'

'Think about it. When did Mark leave? As soon as he saw your tits.'

'He hated my body,' she said.

'Yes, he did.'

'What do *you* think of it?'

'Why do you think I told you to keep your tits covered?'

'Your cock isn't as big as Kieran's,' was the best counter she had.

'Do you wish he was here instead of me?'

She couldn't bring herself to answer that one so she just said, 'Fuck me.'

He increased the speed and force of his thrusts. She was enjoying the feel of his cock going deep inside her every time. He reached around, and finding her clit, rubbed it hard and fast. Her moans were getting louder and more intense. I knew she was going to cum soon. 'Bastard!' she shouted and then came with a scream unlike anything I'd heard from her before.

He just laughed as he let his cock slide out of her. He sat down on the bed and looked at her. It didn't seem to bother him that he hadn't cum. He was satisfied with what he'd done. Tina collapsed onto the bed then sat up again immediately, as if all the emotions churning inside her wouldn't let her rest. She knelt up and reached towards him, making me wonder if she was going to hit him or kiss him. She kissed him. Then she beckoned to me. I came over and she kissed me as well. The three of us sat on the bed together. I realized I was shaking.

'What happened there?' I asked.

'What do *you* think happened?' returned Adam, with a smile.

'I've never seen you cum like that,' I said to Tina. 'Not with Steve, not … ever.' She didn't say anything. She just grinned. 'But that was toxic. It was like you were making hate.'

'I've always said you can have great sex with someone you hate,' said Tina.

'I never thought I'd see it happen, though,' I said. I put my arms around Tina and held her for a moment. 'Why did that turn you on so much?'

She broke away from my embrace to answer. 'I don't know. I got Steve to talk about another woman once. It didn't do much for me.'

'What was different this time?'

Tina thought for a while. 'Well … I know Emma.'

'And you've been jealous of her since you first met her,' said Adam.

'So you knew comparing me to her would drive me crazy.'

'Yes.'

He looked at me. 'This is because of you.'

'How do you figure that?' I asked.

'There's part of you that would love to be the alpha male. You want to be the one who fucks Tina and makes her cum.'

'Well … yes,' I admitted.

'You hate the fact that you'll never do that, so instead you get off on other people doing it. As you develop as a cuckold couple, Tina wants to understand you better. She wasn't ready when she was with Steve, but she is now. Sure, she still wants to be the hottest wife in town. She also gets off on the jealousy.' He turned back to her. 'You want to feel the same as Rob. You want to experience the excitement of being insanely jealous. When Mark ran out on you that night, you were angry, but more than that, you were turned on. You didn't want to hit someone. You wanted to fuck someone.'

'You've got me all figured out,' she said with a thin, sardonic smile. 'I really do hate you.'

He smiled back. 'And when do you want me to fuck you again?'

'You're staying here. You're fucking me tonight and then again in the morning when we wake up.'

'I've got my pajamas and toothbrush in the bag downstairs.'

At that point, I hated him a little bit too.

NEVERTHELESS, WE HAD A pleasant evening. The three of us managed to sit on the couch together. Boris lay across us as if the only thing better than two laps was three. Adam had brought a bottle of Viognier. We drank that while we watched television. When it was time to go to bed, I half expected to be left on the couch. But he made it clear he wanted me to join them.

When we got to the bedroom, he kissed her. It was a long, passionate kiss. Then he said, 'Tina, kiss your husband.'

She came over and kissed me. It was just as long and passionate. She let her robe fall to the floor. Adam and I both undressed quickly. We all lay on the bed together. He kissed her on the lips. Then she turned her head to kiss me. She put her arms behind her head and we both kissed her smooth and sensitive armpits. Adam gazed at her breasts in rapt admiration.

'I thought you hated my tits,' she said.

'Hate is very close to love,' he said, as he covered them with kisses. He started sucking her left nipple. I took her right one into my mouth.

'I've never had them both sucked at the same time before,' she said. 'I thought it would feel twice as good. But it's more like ten times.'

He moved down to her cunt. There was only room for one person between her legs. I locked my mouth against hers. I had to stop kissing her when she gasped. She was feeling something she'd never felt before. I sat up to see what he was doing. With two fingers in her cunt and one a little way up her ass, he was vibrating his fingers inside her. He was also moving his tongue in rapid circles around her clit. After he'd been doing this for less than a minute, her body tensed and she let out a scream. He gently removed his fingers and sat up. When she could breathe normally again, she said, 'Sorry, but that felt *so* good.' It was the first time I'd ever heard a *woman* apologize for cumming too soon.

'Are you okay to carry on?' he asked her.

'Oh yes,' she said.

He took one of my condoms from the bedside table. He didn't need one of Kieran's. Kneeling between her legs, he lifted them up and rested her ankles on his shoulders. He shuffled forward and his cock slipped easily into her cunt. She beckoned me towards her. Surprised, I got on my knees next to her head and she put her lips around my cock. The feel of my cock in her mouth coupled with the sight of another man fucking her two feet away was too much for me. I knew I was about to cum. I tried to pull away, but Tina grabbed the base of my cock and held me in position. 'You're going to let me …?' I asked.

It's not easy to nod when you're lying down with a cock in your mouth, but she managed it. For the first time ever, I felt my wife's soft, warm lips around my cock as I reached my climax. The pleasure and the satisfaction were exquisite as I felt my semen spurting into her mouth. She closed her mouth then opened it again to show me that she'd swallowed it all. I kissed her. I didn't mind the taste of my own cum. I was so grateful and so much in love at that moment. As I was kissing her, she gave a moan of satisfaction. Adam was cumming inside her.

Afterwards, we all lay together. 'Thanks, guys,' she said. 'The problem is I'm not sure I'll ever be satisfied with just one man again.'

That night, the three of us slept in the same bed. Tina lay in the middle. Adam and I lay on either side of her. She told us we could have a breast each. There wasn't much room, so we had to press ourselves tightly against her. None of us seemed to mind.

Chapter Nineteen

~

WE SLEPT LATE THE next morning, until I heard the doorbell ring. I lay still for a moment, hoping it was a dream. It rang again. Tina and I got out of bed, put on our robes, and went downstairs to find Boris by the front door, tail wagging. I looked out the window. 'It's Ben and Emma,' I said.

'Oh no!' said Tina. 'Pretend we're not in.'

'They've seen me.'

'Shit, I'll go upstairs and keep Adam occupied. You get rid of them as soon as you can.'

'Why?'

'I don't want him to meet them,' she hissed, giving me a furious look that I didn't understand.

It was too late. Adam was already coming down the stairs in his pajamas. I had to open the door. They burst in carrying two bottles of champagne. More alcohol! I suspected this lifestyle might break my heart; I didn't realize it would rupture my liver. Emma rushed at me and kissed me on the lips. This was surprising, but not at all unpleasant. 'Thank you so much, Rob,' she said.

'Yes, thank you,' said Ben. 'I don't know what you told my

dad, but we're still married, we've still got our apartment, and I've still got a job.'

'We thought we'd come round and celebrate,' said Emma. 'But … I see you already have company.' She looked at Adam and her eyes widened.

'The new Mr. and Mrs. Jacobs,' he said, shaking them both by the hand. 'Congratulations. I'm Adam.'

For a moment, I wondered if he was actually psychic. Then I remembered their names were on the wedding album.

Emma gave him a knowing look. 'Are you a *friend* of Tina's?'

Tina was still agitated. 'He just came round to drop something off.'

Emma blinked. 'In his pajamas?'

'You said you had to leave first thing, didn't you, Adam?' said Tina, pointedly.

'I never say no to champagne,' he replied. Tina sat down on the couch and looked at the floor. 'We were looking at the wedding photos last night,' continued Adam. 'You looked fantastic, Emma.'

Tina clenched her fists. Emma nodded, as if she already knew how fantastic she looked. I went into the kitchen. We didn't have five matching glasses, but I found some that were close enough.

Back in the den, I sat next to Tina and put my arm around her. Her body was tense.

Ben opened the first bottle. 'Goddess Tina looks like she needs a drink,' Emma told him. 'Are you okay, hon?' Tina nodded briefly. She started to unwind as she drained her first glass and held it out for a refill. 'What did you say to John?' Emma asked me.

'I appealed to his better nature,' I replied.

She narrowed her eyes. 'What did you *really* say?'

'Well …' I looked at Adam.

'You can keep a secret, can't you, Adam?' said Emma.

'I am the silent tomb,' he said, hand on heart.

'So …?' said Emma to me, leaning forward.

'I told him Mark was with Tina that night.'

Emma raised a skeptical eyebrow. 'He believed you?'

'Apparently.'

'Do you know who Mark is?' Emma asked Adam.

Tina snorted. 'Adam knows everything. He's probably worked out your bank account number from the way you're sitting.'

'What do you mean?'

'It's what he does. He reads people.'

Emma looked at Adam, intrigued. 'What do you know about me?'

I breathed a sigh of relief. I was glad we'd got past the question of what I'd told John fairly quickly.

Adam smiled. 'It's Sunday morning. You're dressed like you're going to the opera. Your hair and makeup are perfect. You know you're attractive and you want everyone to see it.'

'Is that all?' asked Emma, wrinkling her nose like she wasn't impressed.

'There's more, but I don't think you want to hear it.'

'Oh, I do.'

'If you're sure ….' He paused, then continued, 'Your father didn't pay much attention to you as you were growing up. He was generous with his money, but not his time. You found yourself an alternative as soon as you could. You've never gone more than a few days without a boyfriend. Sometimes your boyfriends have even overlapped. Ben dotes on you. No one has ever made you feel so adored. And he's rich, so he gives you security, as well. But—sorry about this, Ben—part of you feels he's not good enough for you.'

Ben shrugged. 'I *know* I'm not good enough for her.'

Adam looked at Ben. 'You're from a rich family. You could reasonably expect to marry a beautiful woman. But something happened to shake your confidence.'

'He was born with something that would shake any man's confidence,' said Emma.

'Yes,' said Adam, as if that was obvious. 'You went to an expensive all-boys school.' Ben nodded. 'The other boys were not too polite to mention your—'

'Tiny prick?' prompted Emma.

'It was on the first day,' said Ben. 'We had to shower after football. They said I'd have to marry a hamster because I couldn't satisfy anything else.'

'Was your friend Mark there?'

Ben's face began to crumple as he relived the past. Although his voice caught a few times, he didn't cry. 'I thought he'd … *protect* me. But when I tried to cover myself up, he held my hands behind my back. All the other boys gathered round to laugh at me.'

'You've played that scene in your head a thousand times since then.'

'Of course.'

'Sometimes you see yourself turning into Bruce Lee and flattening all the other boys in the room.'

Ben's upper body tensed as anger replaced sadness. 'That's right.'

'But one time you imagined how different it would have been if all those boys had been girls.'

'How did you—?' began Ben, wide-eyed.

'Told you,' said Tina, a little smug.

'You discovered that you were intensely excited by the thought of girls laughing at you. That set you down the path of trying to find a woman who humiliates you. Now you've found one. She both loves and humiliates you. The perfect package. And Emma, you've found a husband who encourages you to have sex with other men. So you have the continual validation of attracting a string of good-looking studs.'

'Only one since I got married, so far,' said Emma, 'but I'm always on the lookout for the next.'

I felt Tina stiffen beside me. 'Maybe we should have coffee,' I said.

'Actually, we'd better go,' said Emma. 'I'm sure Rob and Tina have a busy day planned. Can we give you a ride, Adam?'

Adam looked at her and smiled. 'Thanks, but I think I'll stay here for a while.'

'We've got more champagne, if you want to carry on talking,' she said, her voice a little silkier. 'Why don't you come home with us?'

'I'm fine.'

Emma looked at him with a mixture of annoyance and disbelief, then stood up. 'Come on, Ben, let's go,' she said. They headed for the door. Before they left, she managed to say, 'Thanks again, Rob.'

There was silence in the den after they'd left. 'You could have gone with them, you know,' said Tina, quietly.

'I prefer it here,' he replied.

She went over and kissed him.

'Didn't you say you wanted me to fuck you before I left this morning?' he asked.

'Definitely,' said Tina. 'Can you leave straight afterwards?' She was already headed for the stairs.

'If you want me to,' he said, rising to his feet.

'I do. Throw me down on the bed. Fuck me senseless. Then fuck off.'

'In that case, we'd better make the arrangements now for when we're going to see each other again. I'd like to come over next Friday and stay the whole weekend.'

I surprised myself by saying, 'Fine by me.'

'And me,' said Tina. 'Now let's go upstairs.'

'Coming, Rob?' said Adam.

'Yes, come on, Rob,' she said. 'Come and watch your wife being used like the fuck-toy she is.'

Chapter Twenty

~

AFTER ADAM LEFT, WE ate pancakes and drank coffee. There was a danger we'd lose the whole day unless we had something inside us to soak up the champagne. Boris sat next to us and enjoyed the pieces of pancake I passed to him. Tina's phone beeped. She looked at the screen and frowned. After reading the message, she handed her phone to me.

Hi Tina, Sorry I haven't been in touch for a while. I've been busy at work. I was wondering if you'd like to get together sometime this week. I'm free on Wednesday, if that's good for you. Hope to see you soon. Kieran

She gave her own interpretation of the message. 'Hi Tina, I've been fucking another woman for a while. But she got bored with the same old thing every time. If you're free on Wednesday, I'd like to come round and get my dick wet.'

'We don't have anything planned for Wednesday,' I said.

'No, we don't.'

She was silent for a couple of minutes, then she typed into her phone. She showed me what she'd written.

Hi Kieran, Unfortunately, we're not around on Wednesday. A lot going on at the moment, so not sure when we'll be available again. Take care. Tina

'That clear enough?' she asked, acid in her tone.

'Set phasers to kill,' I said.

'I don't want to see him again.'

'Even though he does have a huge cock ….'

She thought for a while. 'Yes, but … it would feel wrong.'

'Wrong?'

'Yes, it would feel ….' She suddenly stopped what she was saying and reached for the television control. 'Never mind.'

'No, tell me,' I said, but I could feel my stomach dropping.

'Being with Kieran would feel like … well, it would feel wrong now that I'm seeing Adam.'

'You never want to go with anyone else again?'

'Never say never, but he's the only one I want at the moment.'

We were silent for a long time. I was afraid to ask the next question. 'Tina, how are you feeling about Adam?'

She looked at the floor in silence for a long time. When she lifted her head and looked at me, there were tears in her eyes. 'I'm not sure … but I might be falling in love with him, babe.'

I was even more scared to ask the next question. 'How do you feel about me?'

'I love you with all my heart. That's the problem. I think I'm in love with both of you.'

There was another long silence. Then our eyes met and we said in unison, 'What do we do now?'

www.ingramcontent.com/pod-product-compliance
Lightning Source LLC
Chambersburg PA
CBHW010449100726
47904CB00008B/2538